HIDDEN GODS

Second Endings #4

Lulu M. Sylvian

MOONTAN PRESS

Editing: Michelle Cooper

Cover: Medeiros Creative

Rocks are cool.
Volcanoes are hot.

PROLOGUE

Now Hollywood Report: A recently released exposé from the estate of Hollywood's Golden-age favorite starlet Mancey Heartlove indicates she may have played a bigger role in early communications sciences than originally thought. Previously undiscovered letters hint at a discussion between Heartlove and her friend, the equally glamorous Hedy Lamarr. Implications in these reported letters indicate that Lamarr's signal hopping concept may have originated with Heartlove, but Lamarr saw the big-picture utilization and took the concept to George Antheil to be further developed, with Heartlove's blessing. Lamarr's and Antheil's invention produced varying radio frequencies at irregular intervals for use in military applications, and created the foundations of the technology that would later develop into Wi-Fi signaling, and Bluetooth. Historical reports claim Mancey Heartlove was as giving as she was talented. Rumor or fact, this seems to support her image, even all these decades after her passing.

1

The hanger slid with the sharp rasp of metal on metal as I shoved another handful of clothes to the side.

Ugh, nothing in here was right. Did I own anything that had a glimmer of style, or even trendy fashion to it? The fabric was worn. I may not have a lot of money for new clothes, that wasn't my issue. Without a waistline in sight, everything was vaguely sack-like and covered in floral print in an attempt at being pretty. Everything was frumpy.

'You dressed like this all the time?' I asked. The words were in my head, just as it seemed the presence of Addison Rouche was. Her fashion sense came from a combination of economics, comfort, and lack of self-confidence. I blamed her mother.

I lifted one dress, a shapeless potato sack of a garment with bell sleeves. Addy must have thought it fancy at one point, considering it was a daring glowing magenta with darker tiger like stripes. It looked like the kind of thing someone trying to hide their figure would wear.

The entire wardrobe was full of clothes that hid this

body under a tarp. My closet looked like it belonged to a middle-aged woman.

"How old am I?" I asked the woman sitting in the middle of my bed. She flipped through a photo album as I searched for anything I might be able to salvage before I took the entire lot down to the thrift store and completely replaced all of my clothes.

I took one look at the person who was my mother, and realization dawned. These clothes looked exactly like the things Kristen wore. And she had the kind of domineering personality to run her opinion rough-shod over her daughter.

'*Twenty- six,*' the apparition of Addy said nanoseconds before her mother answered.

"You're twenty-six, Addy."

I grumbled low in my chest. "Please don't call me that."

Kristen sniffed. "But it's your name."

"My name is Addison," I choked out. "I accept that, but I am not Addy. Addy didn't come out of the water. I did."

Just over three months earlier, while on vacation in Hawaii, there had been an accident and Addy had drowned. When the Coast Guard had resuscitated the body I was there, not Addison.

'*I did, too, come out of the water.*'

'*A month ago, Addy. You left me alone in residence for two months.*'

My name is Mancey Heartlove, and once upon a time I was the sweetheart of Hollywood.

"Why do you say such hurtful things?"

It took me a second to regroup. Balancing the two conversations was a challenge when one of us wasn't aware there was a third person in the room. I sat on the bed next to

Kristen, the magenta tiger striped dress still in my grasp. "I'm not saying it to be hurtful."

"You're punishing your father and I for trying to save your marriage." She held open the album and showed me a page of photos. "You were so happy."

The picture showed a couple that were practically total opposites. The man looked old and boney. He was long and thin, with a wispy mustache and small eyes. He looked like a weasel. A dirty trucker cap hid his mangy hair. The woman had a sweetheart shaped face with a short nose, big eyes, and thick, dark hair that hung to her shoulders. She was young and plump. It was a picture of Addy and her ex, Tyler.

In the picture, Addy wasn't smiling. She grimaced through too much makeup. The man next to her didn't have his arm lovingly draped over her shoulders, no, he had a grip on the back of her neck like he was trying to control a dog, or scruff a cat. What the photo didn't show were the bruises.

"I've asked you not to show me pictures of my life with Tyler. You aren't supposed to mention him."

"I just want you to remember who you are."

"Kristen," I started.

"Mom, I'm mom. Don't you remember?" She wiped at tears.

I was getting tired of this same conversation. I should have walked away months ago, but I was having some issues navigating the world. Apparently dying wasn't exactly easy on the body. And Addy didn't have any money. If she had savings, Tyler had taken all of it. I was broke and broken. Staying with Kristen and Bob was the best I could do for now.

When Addy resurfaced into this life, she wasn't exactly forthcoming with the details. I knew Tyler was someone to be avoided. I also knew Addy was desperate for her mother's approval.

I placed my finger over the face of Tyler. "I know he is my ex-husband because you keep telling me. And the only memory I have of him is a gut feeling that he is not good. Addy is not smiling in these pictures, she's faking it, badly."

"Why must you constantly refer to yourself in the third person?" Kristen wailed. She was always so dramatic when she got this way.

I stood and began pinching at the fabric of the dress. Maybe I could take it in, show off the curves that Addy had been trying to hide her entire life. She had a banging body, I should know, I was in it. The curves might have been considered plus size, but the waist to hip ratio this body had was outstanding. As Addy appeared to me she needed a spa day. She had dark circles under her eyes, her hair was typically limp and damp. And the clothes she tended to wear were frumpy at best.

I couldn't keep giving Kristen my focus and attention when she got this way.

In a distracted and disconnected voice I began repeating what the doctors and therapists had told us. "I sustained brain damage when I drowned. I'm very fortunate that my body was able to recover full function considering how long I was under for. I have amnesia, and it's a miracle that all I lost were my memories."

Addy died, but I didn't. I couldn't exactly go around telling people this, especially since it was Addy's body moving around, walking, talking, and Mancey Heartlove had died decades ago in a different century. There was no logic to how I had woken up in her body in a hospital in Honolulu, but I had. Right now my goals were to recover, and get my pasty white ass back to Hawaii.

"But you remember me and Dad," Kristen said.

'I remember you Mom,' Addy said wistfully.

I stopped arguing with Kristen about who I did and didn't remember. I didn't remember her, or the man who was Addy's father. I only knew who she was because she told me. What I remembered was my life in Hollywood, and I remembered my friend Emi in Hawaii. Emi who heard me, and somehow saw me after she had her own brush with death. Emi, who accepted me as her friend while I was nothing more than an organized collection of non-corporeal electrical pulses, a ghost.

And I remembered her brother, Collin. Hubba-hubba, Mr. Sex-appeal on legs. After knowing that men like him existed, why on earth would Addy be interested in returning to that weasel Tyler?

I rubbed the fabric between my fingers, it was all wrong. At first, I thought it felt silky, but now it felt too much like plastic. And while the color was fun, it wasn't worth the effort to remake it into something I might wear. I hung it back with the rest of the clothes. So far, I hadn't found a single thing worth keeping.

I took the photo album from Kristen, and flipped to a page. It was a photo of Christmas a long time ago. Her favorite picture to quiz me over. Her favorite memory of Addy's life.

'I remember that day.' Addy began naming everyone off.

I pointed to the various aunts and grandparents and named them, repeating Addy's words. We had done this many times. I could have named them without Addy's help.

"You remember?" Kristen sounded so excited for a minute.

I shook my head. "No, I have no memory of them, or of this Christmas. I remember their names because you have been drilling them into my head. I understand this Christmas more like a history lesson. I wasn't there, but I've been told about it so often, you really love that story. And to me, it's just that, a story."

"But Addy, it was so romantic. I can't believe you don't remember."

"I was eighteen, I can't believe you thought it was romantic. He was married."

Apparently, Tyler had stormed into the family's big Christmas dinner. And fitting what I learned of him, he was drunk. Kristen considered that a reflection of his deep emotions and not the huge red flag that it was. He grabbed Addy's wrist and dragged her out onto the front lawn, and fell to his knees in the snow and professed his undying love for her. He was pushing thirty at the time and already married. And Kristen thought it was romantic.

'I used to think it was romantic too. I guess I was dumb.'

'Not dumb,' I said in my head. *'Manipulated.'*

A shudder danced down my spine at the thought of it. Addy was a teenager and this older, married man... Well, whatever he thought was going to happen did. They were married as soon as his divorce went through.

A muffled alarm sounded from my phone. I dug through the small pile of clothes I had started on the bed before I realized everything was horrible, and I stopped making a pile. I found it and stopped the noise.

"What's that for?" Kristen asked. Apparently, my newly found habit of setting alarms for appointments was a foreign concept to her.

"I forget things, remember?" The irony of me asking her to remember something was completely lost on her.

"Are you ready to go, Sonny?" Bob, Addy's father, popped his head into the room and asked.

"Yep, let me grab my bag."

"Go where? Why is he calling you Sonny?"

I let out a heavy sigh. "Swimming lessons."

"Addy, swimming? You drowned."

And I hated that fact with a fiery passion. I, Mancey, had made my Hollywood debut as a synchronized swimmer in the aqua chorus of many MGM films before being discovered and launching skyward to becoming one of Hollywood's sweethearts. "Yeah, and I never want that to happen again. Try calling me Sonny. I'm trying a different nickname, to see if it fits me better. I'm not Addy, and I'm not sure if I'm Addison."

Kristen gasped. "Sonny? No, you're my Addy. Next, you'll want me to use pronouns."

I closed my eyes and took in a deep breath through my nose. I didn't have time for a grammar lesson.

2

One, two, three, breathe. I gasped in a lung full of fresh air and put my face back in the water. Not breaking the even pace of my strokes. I stopped circling my arms and left them outstretched as I approached the end of the lane. My hand hit the wall. I folded my knees up to my chest, rolled, and rotated. I pushed off the wall and began kicking.

At the end of my lap, I braced my elbows on the edge of the pool. I wiped water from my face and scanned the deck for my swimming instructor. My eyes found him, he had hunkered down at the edge of the pool and was speaking to another swimmer in the water.

He looked up and saw me watching them. With a flick of his wrist, he told me to take another lap. He was waiting for me when I returned. I held onto the ledge as he squatted down to my level.

"I don't understand why you think you need swimming lessons," he said.

I wiped water from my face. "I want to be certain of my skills," I replied. "I don't want to be afraid of the water."

"It was a freak accident, kiddo, I think it's safe to say you've got this."

"Are you kicking me out of lessons?" I asked. I didn't want to stop swimming. I felt at ease in the pool. Addy left me in peace for a few hours. And I really did delight in how it shocked the people who know about the accident. *But you drowned, why are you swimming?*

"What, and turn down your monthly fees?" he chuckled. "Maybe if I had a waiting list, but I don't. You're welcome in my class. I think you really just need some minimal coaching at this point. I'm graduating you to the lanes next week." He pointed to the other side of the pool, where floats divided a section of the pool into lanes. The people who swam there just did laps, they didn't get lessons.

I started to open my mouth to protest.

"You can always ask me questions, but I don't think you need me to guide you every step of the way. You leveled up, you should be proud of yourself."

"Do I have time to do a couple of more laps?" I asked as we both glanced up at the clock. If I timed this right, I could swim until the next class of little kids was ready to climb in the pool. That way, I didn't have to deal with the children or their mothers at the same time I wanted to get dressed.

The dressing room was nothing more than a few benches in a wide-open locker room. There was no privacy. I wasn't particularly shy, but the comments out of little kid's mouths frequently were parroting the not so nice things their parents said in the car, or while talking to other adults. I wasn't a small woman. The size of my curves did not need to be the topic of anyone's conversations. I certainly didn't need to hear how big my butt was coming out of the mouth of a four-year-old. I had a feeling Addy had listened entirely too often to those comments. Between the trauma of the dressing room, and the water itself, she made herself scarce during swim classes.

I finished my laps, and sat on the edge of the pool while I watched the little kids dance their way out of the dressing room and onto the pool deck. With the kids at poolside, that meant the moms— the people I was really avoiding— would be out of the changing room.

I got to my feet and dripped my way into the room. I didn't bother wrapping up in a towel, it only became a soaking wet blob for me to haul around afterward. The changing room was blessedly empty except for another woman from my class. She was the one who told me the trick of waiting until the kids were climbing into the pool strategy before changing.

I wrapped a towel around my body and began shimmying out of my suit.

"Addison, is that you? Addison? Jesus, Addison, you don't have to be so rude."

I didn't turn until a clammy hand dropped onto my shoulder.

I turned with a gasp. I acted like I was plucking those expensive little earphones out of my ears. "Sorry, I didn't hear you."

I had heard her, only I had a bad habit of not responding to the name Addison. I was Mancey and having a hard time remembering that other people didn't know that. It was no different from someone calling me Sherry or Olive. I wasn't going to think they were talking to me because it wasn't my name.

"Addison, don't you remember me? I didn't believe Tyler when he said you got amnesia. You know all of that's fake. So did he finally leave you for a younger model?"

For once, I really wished Addy had decided not to ghost

around swimming lessons. I could use a little help identifying this person.

She raked her eyes down my figure and back up to my face.

I gave her my brightest audition smile. "I'm Addison, right? I keep forgetting. Tyler who?"

The other woman rolled her eyes and shook her head. "You are so faking it."

That's when I stopped acting. I scrunched up my face and cocked my head to the side. "Yeah, I'm really sorry, but I don't remember you. If you talked to Tyler, then he probably told you way too much or not enough about the accident."

"So, you do know Tyler?"

"I know who he was to me, but I don't actually have any active memories of him. And I'm sorry, but this is really personal, and I don't know you." I put up my hand and took a step backward to get away from her, essentially putting my body into the cubby where my clothes hung.

She sniffed and looked down her nose at me. "You're faking it. I can tell. I wish I had thought about having amnesia after that asshole left me for you. Maybe I should pretend to not know him, either."

I squinted hard at her. She was in her mid-to-late thirties, but probably younger than that. She looked tired, and tired people tended to look older than they were.

"Momma, can I go out there now?" the kid with her asked.

"Yes, git, you're already late." She shooed her daughter out toward the pool.

"I'm not sure what Tyler told you, but—"

"He said he got knocked into the water and actually died for a minute, and then you had to pretend you hit your head. And when you woke up, you started acting funny. Like you didn't know him. He said it was all some ploy to keep him from divorcing you."

I simply shook my head. From what I knew of Tyler, he was a cheat clearly, and I suspected an abuser. And this was proof positive he was a liar. Of course, I couldn't state for certain that he hadn't been unconscious when they pulled him from the water. I had no memories of that moment, just the stories from my parents.

"Did he hit you?" I asked.

Her eyes went wide, and she quickly glanced around the changing room. "How dare you!"

"Did he hit you?" I repeated. "I think he hit me." I licked my lips, and chewed on the lower one for a second before continuing. "I don't have any memories from the time of the accident and before. And I am very sorry that Addison's actions in the past caused you any pain. You shouldn't believe anything that man says, after all, he somehow convinced the family of an eighteen-year-old that it was romantic of him to leave his wife and demand that a child marry him."

She scoffed loudly. "That's rich, you calling yourself a child. You had been fucking him for at least a year, if not longer."

"And that's concerning," I said. "Whoever I was got left behind with the accident. And the stories Addison's mother—"

"You mean your mother," she corrected.

"The stories she tells me about how romantic it all was turns my stomach. So, again, I am sorry for the part Addison played in the past. But that's not me. I see you have a beautiful daughter now, so I hope that means you moved on from Tyler and found someone better."

She jerked her head back and looked confused, her brow crinkled, and her nose scrunched up. "Who are you, and what have you done with Addison?"

I let out one of those stress laughs. No one was going to believe the truth. "I don't know, and it's freaking a lot of people out."

I knew who I was, I just didn't know how to be who I really was while trying to navigate being Addison.

Addison's father waited by his sedan out in the parking lot.

My wet hair dripped onto my shoulders. I didn't want to be in that changing room a moment longer than necessary. The entire encounter with Tyler's first wife had felt like an ambush. And talking to strangers who thought they knew me was never something that I had been particularly good at, even during my Hollywood days. At least during those encounters I had the right memories to fall back on, and I faked it well.

Addy could have been more helpful, but she never seemed to be around when I could use her help. I was quiet as Bob drove us back to the house. I watched the town flash past the windows, the place that was supposed to be home, but held no memories or emotions.

He pulled the car alongside the mailbox and reached in. He shuffled through the mail on his lap before handing it over to me. "It looks like you got something official there."

I sorted through the mail as he pulled into the drive. One long, business sized envelope looked like a check, and a second small envelope with calligraphy on the front, both addressed to me.

I ripped into the smaller envelope first. The only hint I had was the cancelled stamp from Hawaii. I stamped my feet and did a happy little dance in my seat.

"Good news?" Bob asked.

"My friend Emi is getting married," I practically squealed. I couldn't wait to see her again, and a wedding meant her brother Collin would be there.

"Is she some girl you went to high school with?"

I really didn't have the words that would let people know how I knew Emi without making it sound like I was losing my mind. "I think so."

3

"Your hair is wet," Kristen complained as soon as I walked in the door. "You'll catch a cold."

I ignored her and muttered about taking a shower. Between the mailbox and front door I realized that even if I could convince Bob and Kristen that I had known Emi, and they had just never met her, it didn't mean there was money to fly me to Hawaii for the wedding.

Kristen liked to point out how much I was costing them with my medical and therapy bills. It wasn't my fault the insurance payout hadn't come through yet.

I took a shower, wrapped up in a towel, and walked back into my bedroom. I let out a heavy sigh. All the clothes that I had pulled from the closet to donate were back on hangers.

Addison had no autonomy. No wonder she looked defeated every time I saw her.

I opened the folding closet door and gasped.

"What are you doing in there?" I asked. We were alone, so I spoke outloud.

Addy stepped out of the back of the closet. "I used to

hide in there, in the dark, behind everything. There's enough space to curl up."

"You used to hide in your closet as a kid? Why?" I had a good idea why. But did Addy? Would she even admit it? Changing the topic, I asked, "Why are all the clothes back in the closet?"

"Mom put my clothes away."

"Do you even like these clothes? It doesn't matter. I just spent over an hour clearing everything I will not wear out, and she just puts it all back?" I grumbled as I got dressed. If Kristen had undermined Addison like she had been doing to me, no wonder Addy had accepted attention from Tyler. He probably made her feel accepted for the first time in her life.

"Well, this is bullshit. I'm going to go talk to her about it."

"No, don't. She'll get mad," Addy pleaded.

"Let her."

I crossed the house looking for Kristen. She was curled up in a corner on the couch in the living room. Her chihuahua, tucked up in the crook of her legs, shivered and growled at me. The weather channel was on. She watched it like it was a soap opera. The drama of a major storm cell across the midwestern plains was apparently fascinating to her.

"Why did you put all those clothes back?" I demanded.

"I think you mean, thank you," she snapped.

"No, I don't mean, thank you. I mean, why did you undo all the work I had just done? I was going to donate all of those clothes. Now I need to go through everything again."

She swatted lightly at the growling dog. "Stop it. Don't growl at Addy. I don't know what's going on with him."

He knew I wasn't Addison, that's what was going on.

'*He's never liked me,*' Addison said. '*He doesn't like anyone but Mom.*'

'*That makes even more sense,*' I replied inside my head.

"He's never liked me," I said out loud.

Kristen sat up a little. "You remembered?"

I shook my head. "He doesn't even like Bob. It's obvious." I wasn't going to give her a false sense of hope. "So, why did you do it?"

"I'm your mother, I was putting your clothes away. You threw a fit. I cleaned up after you. Like I always do."

I let out a derisive laugh. "You think that was me throwing a fit?"

My voice pinched in my throat, winding my tone to a higher pitch. If that woman wanted to see what it looked like when I threw a fit, I was ready to oblige.

'*Mancey. Stop,*' Addy pleaded.

I stopped. I huffed air through my nose. "Next time, please do not put anything back into the closet without checking with me first."

"You weren't here, what did you expect me to do?" Kristen asked.

"Leave my stuff alone."

"Don't talk to me that way. How dare you disrespect me in my own home?" She jumped to her feet. The dog scampered to the opposite side of the couch and continued to growl.

"How dare you undo all the work I put into cleaning out that closet?" I wasn't intimidated, and I wasn't going to back down.

Addy on the other hand was completely cowed. '*Please Mancey, stop.*'

"That's it, you're grounded. Go to your room."

I snorted out a laugh. "You can't ground me."

I was about to tell her she wasn't my mother when Addy's electric shock of a touch buzzed along my arm where she had grabbed me. She shook her head frantically.

"Fine." I spun on my heel and stormed through the kitchen and out the back door, leaving Kristen sputtering.

'You don't have to antagonize my parents so much.'

'I wasn't antagonizing anyone. I was standing up for myself. Something you might think about doing from time to time.'

I continued stomping my way across the yard and into the old garage. It was a separate out building that was probably more tool shed than meant to keep a car in. In all of my time at their house, I hadn't yet explored out here.

I opened the door and groaned. To nobody's surprise, it was a dump. Tools and equipment were piled on top of each other. There was barely a path through stacks of old paint cans to the far side of the space. The windows were coated in dust and cobwebs, giving the light a greasy orange haze quality.

"What is this place?"

"Dad used to putter around in here when I was little. I was never allowed back here. It's dangerous. We probably shouldn't go in."

Too late, I was already knee-deep in the broken lawn mowers and boxes, and headed toward what looked like had once been a very organized peg board of hand tools. The bench in front was piled high with random bits of hardware, the tools that were never returned to their spot on the board, and wires.

Wires?

Now that looked out of place. The yard working equipment, and the handyman construction tools made perfect sense. But that wire was wrapped in blue plastic and was plugged into a wiring harness. I tugged, trying to see if there was an easy way to get to the other end of this thing.

Hand tools spilled onto the floor. I jumped out of the way, preserving my toes.

"There's radio equipment in here," I announced.

"Yeah, Dad used to do that. I think. Like I said, I was little and not allowed in here."

I cast a quick gaze around the place. The light was fading, and I hadn't found a light switch yet. "Let's come back tomorrow, see what we can do."

"But Mom grounded you. I mean us."

I laughed. "It's not like either of us can go anywhere without Bob or her driving. I doubt she'll be too upset if we're out here. It's infinitely more interesting than watching the weather channel and having that mutt growl at me all day."

I brushed my hands off on the thighs of my jeans before heading back into the house.

"There's my girl," Bob said as I came back in. "Go wash up, your mother has dinner ready."

I tried not to cringe at his blatant attempts at affection. It felt forced, like he wasn't used to expressing his emotions. I also wasn't convinced he meant any of it. Maybe he was feeling guilty about his part of the accident. Not that I knew what it was, but I figured there was so much more to the story than what I had been told.

"What's for dinner?" I asked.

"Your favorite," Kristen chimed in with a pleasant tone, as if we had not been bickering earlier.

'Spaghetti!' Addy said.

"Spaghetti?" I repeated.

"Not spaghetti," Kristen said with a shake of her head.

She did not hide the sneer that crossed her face. Clearly, she wasn't a fan of spaghetti. "Lasagna."

'Ew, no. She always puts too much zucchini in it.'

"Zucchini does not belong in lasagna," I replied.

"You really don't remember, you love my lasagna."

Even if I didn't have Addy over my shoulder with a running commentary on how much she did not like zucchini or her mother's lasagna, I did not need the prompt to complain myself.

The next morning, I was up and dressed and out in the tool shed before anyone had a chance to pester me about what I was going to do today. It was always an uncomfortable conversation.

Addy had no education, and for the jobs she was qualified to work, well I couldn't see how any hiring manager was going to accept that I both had amnesia, and could run a cash register.

Besides, it was Kristen who was pushing me to get a job, when I was under clear instructions from the lawyers not to go to work. It had something to do with the settlement they were working on getting for me.

I doubted I would ever see any of that money. But as long as the doctors agreed I shouldn't be working just yet, I was fine not subjecting myself to the interview process again.

Kristen paid about as much attention to the doctor's and lawyer's instructions as she did to me. It was as if she knew what was best for everyone and no one else's opinion or expertise mattered. I knew movie stars with smaller egos.

"It's gross and dusty in here. And there are bugs," Addy announced after I had waded through the detritus in the garage back to the workbench.

"You can't get dirty, and bugs can't bite you, relax."

"Why are we here anyway?"

"I saw old radio parts. I wanted to see if I could get them working."

"As if you would know how to do that."

"I have a degree in engineering. I know exactly how to do that." I stopped myself before I directed her to flip the switch at the end of the table. I hoped it would power up the lights. "Excuse me." I leaned over and was happy to discover the switch did turn the lights on.

With better illumination, I began digging through the treasure trove the bench was proving to be. As much as I wanted to sweep everything off and start with a clean table, I methodically began aligning tools onto the peg board. I spent hours cleaning and organizing.

At some point, Addy flitted away. She was bored watching me rediscover my scientific roots before I became an actress.

I spent the next several days cleaning and playing in the garage. I giggled like a child at Christmas when I found a soldering set up, complete with flux and wire. It was even more fun when the soldering iron actually got hot after plugging it in.

It was a few more days before I had anything that resembled a radio together. I had a speaker that produced static, and knobs that turned, but it was all pretend as far as functionality goes.

"Addiso-Sonny, are you in here?" Bob called out from the door.

"Back here," I called back.

"What have you been up to? It's dangerous back here..." his voice trailed off as he saw the tidy and organized work area I had created. Addy followed him in.

"I was bored, and I figured Kristen wouldn't come back

here and undo everything I was trying to do." I had effectively given up on cleaning out the clothes I was never going to wear. They could just take up closet space, since that seemed too important to Addy's mother.

"How'd you... what in tarnation?"

I gestured at the phone. "YouTube. They show you how to do everything on there."

I had that little lie lined up for just this situation. I couldn't say I had learned from him, since there was no way this family would let their daughter do anything other than wifey type activities. And I couldn't imagine that Kristen was a very good teacher when it came to the culinary and house-keeping arts.

"Did you get it to work?" Bob leaned in and examined the radio receiver.

Addy showed interest in what I was doing for the first time since I started. She reached out to touch the radio.

Static buzzed and popped from the speaker.

I quickly cut my gaze to Addy. My heart pounded in my throat.

"What was that? A signal?" Bob asked as he began fiddling with the knobs.

'What? Why are you staring at me like that?'

'Touch it again,' I directed Addy.

'It's not like I did anything.'

"Did anything," sounded faintly, and very broken up through the speakers.

"Do it again!" I said out loud in my excitement.

Bob grunted and more studiously fiddled with it.

'Touch the radio and say something,' I directed Addy.

'Like this?' Her hand was firmly on the device, but not even static came out.

I sighed. "Well, it worked for a second."

"Keep at it, maybe you'll actually get this darned thing to work. I never could." Bob set the radio down. "Time to come inside. Your mother sent me to find you. It's dinner time."

"I'll be right there," I said as he waded through his junk and back out the door.

I stared at the old radio. Had I managed to get a signal from Addy? She was a form of energy, why not? I wanted to run more experiments. I needed Addy to touch the radio while I made adjustments, but she was already out the door and following her father inside the house.

I switched off the light and gingerly navigated through the piles. During all the time I spent in the garage, I had given the path very little attention.

I washed up and made my way to the table.

Kristen and Bob were already seated, and looking at me expectantly. The table was set as if this were a fancy meal. Plates were flanked with forks on one side and knives and spoons on the other. Kristen typically just plated up food and tossed forks on the table— knives and spoons only came out when needed.

"What?" I asked.

Kristen gestured at the envelope displayed across my empty plate. "It's from the lawyer. Open it. What does it say?"

I was surprised she hadn't already sliced it open. Maybe she had and glued it back together, and that's why she was so excited.

I sat down before picking up the letter and the butter knife from my place setting.

"Well?" she asked eagerly before I even slipped the letter out.

I kept everything neatly folded together. If there were any surprises in here, I didn't want her to find out about them. I had been very protective of my case with the lawyers and insurance companies.

I scanned over the letter. Thank God I was a decent actor. I was an excellent poker player because my face never gave away any emotion unless I wanted it to. I was a crappy poker player because I never quite got the cards to work in my favor, but I won through expert bluffing.

All of my poker and acting skills were in use at the moment. I folded the letter back up and put it in the envelope.

"Addison, what does it say?" Kristen asked again.

"It's just an update on the proceedings. I'm not going to be needed for an additional deposition. And they expect a ruling soon."

That's not what the letter said at all.

"I'll need a ride into town next week," I said to Bob. "They are sending someone with some papers for me to sign from their main office."

"How much money are we getting?" Kristen asked. She was always more interested in how big my potential payout was going to be.

I shook my head and shrugged. "I'm not very hungry right now. I think I'll eat later."

I excused myself and left.

"They must not be paying her anything. Did you see how disappointed she is?" I could hear Kristen bitching at Bob. "We should sue."

"Kristen," Bob responded. "She is suing, that's what that letter is all about."

I closed my bedroom door so I could no longer hear them talking about me, and the money I was to be awarded, as if it were their money.

I pulled the letter back out as I sat on the edge of the

bed. I hadn't told Kristen what this letter was about at all. She was so grabby when it came to the finances of my accident, I really did not want her involved. And if she knew exactly how much money was involved, she would find a way to get it from Addison. I knew she would.

But she wasn't dealing with Addy, she was dealing with me. And I knew how to manage my own assets.

I blew air out through pursed lips. I hadn't lied when I told Bob I needed a ride into town to sign papers. I just hadn't mentioned it was to get my check. And it was going to be a very large one. I had signed some impressive contracts in my time, but even when I was at the top of my starlet game, I had never seen so many zeros on the left side of the decimal point.

I looked up and stared at the open closet full of clothes that hurt my fashion heart. I didn't need to sort through anything. I could afford to get rid of it all and start from scratch. More importantly, I could afford to go to Emi's wedding in Hawaii, traveling first class, even.

4

———

Everything felt so familiar, yet so different.

Emi, now the Emmy-nominated-for-best-supporting-actress Emi Paul, had spent months recovering from a near fatal accident in this backyard. But today it barely resembled the location of her convalescence. As far as yards went, it was fairly well-kept up, but it hadn't been maintained by a professional gardener.

By sheer fact of location on Maui, it was a thousand times more verdant and luxuriant than the backyard I had left behind in Idaho. Clearly, professionals and additional plants had been brought in to amplify the level of lush. Strings of fairy lights sparkled, and torches strategically placed around the perimeter warded off a majority of the bugs.

It was a backyard worthy of a cinematic production. It took the natural beauty of the location, expanded and enhanced it. I was well familiar with scene settings that took a near perfect place and made it unworldly with a level of perfection that nature could never meet. Of course, Emi was in the industry, it didn't surprise me in the least.

Chairs were lined up in rows for us to watch the ceremony. Emi was such a natural beauty, she could have worn a potato sack and looked stunning. Her dress was a gossamer delight in sparkling gold tones. She shimmered. While I should have been paying attention to her and her husband, Jeremy, I was having a hard time keeping my gaze from lingering on her brother, Collin.

The first time I met him, he didn't meet me, after all, I had been non-corporeal at the time. But he had been very real, very solid, very... hmmm, so very masculine even though his golden bronze skin had glowed as if he was coated in glitter. I later found out that he frequently did sparkle with a coating of shimmering glitter lotion, but that was saved for performances. No, Collin had refracted a dazzling display of light naturally.

He had lured me in like an angler fish in the dark. He was the light I had gravitated toward. As if I had finally found the end of my after-life tunnel. Only, instead of finding myself in Collin Paulo's company, I had found myself in this body. I was pasty pale, and even though I had only been in Hawaii a few days, I was losing ground in the battle of sunscreen versus the sun. The tops of my shoulders and the tip of my nose were sunburned pink.

I had to admit defeat and find a shawl to drape over my shoulders for this event. At least the insurance money had come in, and I was able to buy myself clothes that were fashionable and not disrespectful toward this body.

Addison's mother hated everything I selected when I asked her to take me shopping for this trip.

"That shows off your... tummy," she complained. And if it wasn't the tummy, it was the butt.

There had been lots of disappointed sighing on that excursion.

Addy hadn't been much help either. She was completely cowed around her mother. Even as a ghost she deferred to the other woman. Addy only ever showed a modicum of backbone when her mother was nowhere around.

"Wearing a floral tent isn't going to magically change the shape of this body," I said. I had been standing in a lovely, rather curve conforming dress. It was a bit slinky with femme fatale vibes. I thought it looked sexy on my new body. And the particular shade of blue enhanced my eyes like crazy.

"You look fat," Kristin scoffed.

'Mom's right, I'm not comfortable dressed like that,' Addy commented.

'I didn't ask you, and you aren't the one wearing it, I am.'

"Well, this body is fat," I admitted. "But I can still dress it without having to try to hide it. I think this dress looks good."

Kristin let out a heavy sigh. The way that woman could use her breath to convey her levels of disappointment was something I had never experienced with an adult. I had known plenty of teenagers who had struggled to use their words and instead used sighs, whimpers, and moans to convey meaning.

"What?" I snapped. "What's so wrong with wanting to look good?"

She grimaced. "But does showing off your size really look good?" There it was. Kristin was the kind of person who thought larger bodies needed to be hidden. How much did she hate herself, because she wasn't a smaller person either? How much self-confidence damage had she done to poor Addison?

"Well, I like it, and I'm the one who will be wearing it.

I'm getting it." I bought the dress and insisted that Kristin take me home.

The drive home had been uncomfortable. Between her silence, or her lecturing me over dressing properly for my shape. All of Addison's clothes suggested she was shaped like a manatee, a blob with a cute face. But Addison's body, my body, had curves. I was shaped like a classic hourglass, just plus-sized. I saw no reason to hide the incredible waist to hip ratio she had.

So there I was standing off to the side at Emi's wedding in a dress that did just that, it emphasized the curve of my hips. But not so to the point where it looked like I was trying to take attention away from the bride. Which was impossible on a day like today, she was beyond stunning in her wedding gown with her glorious dark hair in a half up half down style.

It would have taken so much more effort to upstage Emi than I had been willing to put in. And I had been a Hollywood starlet. I knew how to upstage. Today, I didn't want to pull everyone's attention away from Emi. I just wanted one man to look at me, Collin.

'On my God, is everyone here famous?' Addy asked with a nervous quaver to her voice. She practically vibrated next to me.

Even as a ghost, she was able to change her choice of fashion, and she had dressed in what she thought was more appropriate for a wedding. She had the same body shape as I did, yet, she looked like a floral feed bag. It was the dress her mother had preferred.

'I told you, Emi works in television.'

'I know, but I didn't think you meant she was a TV star. Oh whoa, is that Liam James? He's so hot.'

If Addy had any volume to her voice, that would have

stopped all conversations and people would have stared. I wiggled my finger in my ear to recover. Fortunately, her celebrity panic went straight into my brain.

'That's George O'Connell!' Addy practically screamed.

'Are you going to name every single person here?'

'I don't know everyone here, but he's walking this way.'

The man Addy was freaking out about was movie star handsome— taller than average, but not towering. He had a square jar, a strong nose, a broody brow, and his salt and pepper hair was cut short and brushed to the side like a news channel anchorman. If he was going to talk to me, it was time to dust off my vamping skills and see if I was still good at the flirting thing. I could use a test run before approaching Collin.

"I don't think we've met," George O'Connell, Mr. Suave Hollywood himself, sauntered up to me. His gaze scanned over me like a rake over hot coals, looking for a spark.

Something inside of me shivered. It was nice to be appreciated.

'Did he just check you out?' Addy became a quivering pile of goo over George O'Connell.

I knew his type entirely too well. If I was still a starlet, I would have hooked myself to him with hopes of becoming a Hollywood power couple. The kind of couple that studios put together on screen and off. My dark hair and pale coloring would have paired nicely with his not quite silver-fox, tanned appearance.

"I know who you are, Mr. O'Connell. It's a pleasure to meet you." I held my hand out, palm down.

He took the cue and kissed the back of my knuckles as I batted my eyelashes at him. I really hoped Collin was watching, and getting jealous.

I hadn't been introduced to him yet this afternoon, but it

never hurt to have a little precedence of desirability established. I couldn't have asked for a better endorsement than obvious flirting from a star like George O'Connell. This wedding party was full of actors. Talk about familiar, and yet, I shouldn't have been too comfortable here. After all, Addison was not an actress. Addison had been a nobody in her own life. I was going to change that.

"You have me at a disadvantage. You know who I am through my work, but I cannot place you. You aren't from the Johnny Urban cast, are you? It's practically a show reunion here today. You seem familiar." His voice was a deep rumble, practically a purr. His eyes sparkled, and I swear a spark flashed off his perfectly white teeth. The man knew what he was doing.

'He's talking to you!' Addy gasped. For a person who didn't breathe, her interpretation of someone hyperventilating was spot on.

"We haven't worked together, I'd remember you." George gave me another appreciative scan.

I laughed. I wanted to say, 'Oh honey, you must try harder than that. I dated Errol Flynn.' But I couldn't be Mancey here. Instead, I blushed, it was surprisingly easy.

"I think I might be the only one here not from Hollywood. No, I'm not an actress. I, uhm, I—" I shot my gaze around the party quickly looking for a light bulb of an idea.

My eyes locked with Collin's. I felt it like a hand wrapping around the back of my neck in a possessive hold. His dark eyes went wide, and I got my flash of inspiration.

"Oh, you're from the groom's side?" George lifted one brow and gave me a half smile. He was attractive, and damned charming. But he didn't have the *je ne sais quoi* that oozed and roiled around Collin.

"No, no. I'm a graduate student at the University of Hawaii. I actually met Emi during her convalescence."

"You're a local?" I could see George trying to work out those details.

"Not exactly. I'd love to move here. Emi and I really bonded before, and I missed her like a sister when I had to go home. But"— I waved my hand in the air, dismissing the thought.

"Oh no, you can't just drop the story right as it gets interesting. Where is home, and why did you have to leave?"

"Idaho," I said. "My mother insisted, though I think staying here after the divorce would have proven to be far more interesting... Oof!"

A small body slammed into me before I gave away too much information that should have felt personal, but didn't because it didn't feel like my personal information.

"Hamilton!" I exclaimed as I reached down and lifted him up.

He squirmed in my arms. "Put me down."

"You don't remember me, do you?" Of course, he didn't, I didn't look like Mancey at all. "Are you looking for frogs?"

His little eyes went wide and he stopped wiggling. "How did you know?"

"Because the edge of the yard is the best place for them." I set him down. "Let me know if you find any," I called out after him as he ran away.

"You know her stepson too?"

"He doesn't remember me," I said as I twisted my face up. I couldn't keep acting as if I were me, and still hold up the Addison life. "I have a question for you, Mr. O'Connell."

"George," he corrected.

I smiled. "Okay, George. How do you reconcile your

characters with who you are?" I tapped him in the middle of his chest.

"That's far too deep of a question for a beautiful day like today. You're serious?"

I nodded. "I don't feel like me sometimes."

"Oh, George, there you are." A middle-aged woman, who clearly spent her time and money in spas to maintain her beauty, approached us. She was beautiful, her money was well invested. "I've been looking for you everywhere. I need you to come help me sell Liam on doing another television series."

George held out his arm, and the woman slid in next to him, so that they were standing there with his arm around her waist.

"Sunny, meet... I guess I never did catch your name," George said to me.

I looked into Sunny's sharp eyes, and did not miss the way they were narrowed in my direction. She did not approve of George speaking to me for reasons of her own. At that moment, I knew that playing around with the name Sonny wasn't going to work for me. I didn't want to match her energy in any way.

"Pleasure, darling. Come George." Sunny pulled George before I was ever able to give him my name.

But what name would I have given him? I wasn't Sonny, that was clear now. And I didn't want to be Addy, I didn't want her memories or her past. I was pretty sure she didn't want her past either, she just didn't know how to get away from it.

5

———

I watched George and Sunny for a moment before scanning the crowd. I was looking for someone.

'He was flirting with you. A man like that would never,' Addy gasped. She sounded like a fish out of water. That was not a pleasant sound.

'A man like that absolutely would, unless you're wearing a feed sack.' I made sure she knew I gave her one of those checking her out looks.

'But Mom said this was a good dress.'

'Addison, your mom doesn't like you.'

'Shut up, she loves me.' And in a poof of indignation, she was gone. Good.

I didn't need her third wheeling it as I tried to catch my man. I just needed to find him again.

I hissed in a sharp breath of air when my gaze finally found who I was looking for. "Damn, there are three of them."

Three large slabs of human male yumminess, fit for consumption. And I wanted to consume. Well, one of them at least. It was as if each one was taller, more profoundly fit, and a more exemplary specimen of Pacific Islander masculinity than the other. My head was spinning.

While George was taller than average, he fit into the crowd. These three men towered over the rest of Emi's guests. Each one was broader through the shoulders than the one before. And that was intimidating, considering one of them had been a professional football player. So much chest, so much shoulder, so many muscles.

As distracting as the other two men were, my gaze was steady on my target, Collin. Of the three, he was the shortest. To say Collin was short was a fallacy. He was just not the tallest in a small cluster of gigantic men. The tallest was his brother, Brand, the ex football player. They looked entirely too much alike to not be related. With chiseled features, jaws of granite, deep tanned skin, and black hair. Brand wore his hair in long locks. Collin wore his in a conservative, short, slicked back style that was fitting since he was a college professor.

Brand and Collin were Emi's brothers. And that's how I knew who they were, even though I had never officially met either. They were both included in the ceremony and wore official wedding party colors. Finding suits in her color theme that fit over their bulging muscles had to have been a challenge. I didn't know who the third man was. Emi had only told me about two brothers. Maybe he was a cousin? He was as delicious as the others with the same coloring and long thick hair pulled back in a half knot with the back hanging down, not unlike the same style Emi wore.

Now that I had identified my quarry, I needed to act. My insides wanted to riot. What the hell was that? Me, nervous? I was a Hollywood starlet once upon a time. Men were nervous around me, not the other way around. Then again, that had been a different lifetime, and a different body.

I smoothed my hands across my middle and down over my hips. What was I worried about? George fucking O'Connell had been flirting with this version of me. If I could snag a man like that, then Collin Paulo, a nerdy college professor should not be a challenge for my feminine wiles, he should be drinking champagne from my shoe by the end of the evening.

With a steadying breath, I stepped forward.

"You're Addison, right?" A slender redhead stopped me.

"Sort of," I responded without thinking. I hated not feeling myself with that name, yet that was the name for this body. "You're Emi's sister-in-law, aren't you? The writer?"

"More like illustrator, yeah, that's me. Gil." She stuck out her hand.

We shook, and then she wrapped her arm around my elbow. "Emi told me about you. I wanted you to meet my husband, Brand. You haven't met the brothers yet, have you?"

I shook my head. This time, when the nerves in my insides clenched, I needed to know just what Emi had told this woman.

"You, Emi, and Brand are all in a rather unique club," Gil continued as she led me away from the edge of the yard.

I raised my brows and stared at Gil. I would have preferred it to be just one eyebrow, but I could not get the muscles in this forehead to behave.

She glanced up at me as I slowed. "My husband also had a near death accident."

"Ah, yes. That's not one of those things I go around advertising," I admitted.

"But it's how you met Emi, during her recovery from her accident," Gil confirmed.

I nodded. As long as Emi didn't go around announcing

we met while I was non-corporeal, I didn't see why either of us should lie about when we met. The how would need some nuance in its explanation. My heart fluttered as we approached the group of men who I had been focused on. I felt Collin's presence like a fine electrical buzzing over my skin.

"Brand, this is Emi's friend, Addison, the one she was telling us about," Gil introduced us.

Up close, the men were physically intimidating as hell. I shook Brand's hand. It was large, his handshake firm, and his skin was warm. "Nice to meet you. This is my brother, Collin."

Collin simply nodded at me.

The third man tapped his fingers against his shades in a salute before waving. Even though his eyes were hidden behind a pair of dark aviators, I sensed the touch of his gaze over all of me. "Brody. You can call me Bro. And unironically, I'm the one not related."

"So, everyone is a brother here," I laughed.

"Yeah, I guess so," Collin said, dryly. His voice was low, without inflection, and he let out a grunt of a harrumph with his judgment.

"You need to lighten up. It's not that serious." Bro slapped Collin on the back of his shoulder.

"Oh good, Mancey, you're meeting everybody," Emi appeared as if from thin air. She wrapped her arms around her brothers' waists and squirmed in between them.

She was so tiny compared to her brothers. They were both very sturdy and grounded, human mountains. But Emi was a flier. Unlike my accident, where I drowned, I was allowed back in the water if I wanted. Unfortunately, Emi was not supposed to do her aerial silks anymore.

"I thought you just said your name was Addison?" Collin asked.

I stammered. I didn't have a ready answer.

"Oh, crap, my bad. I forgot," Emi spoke quickly.

"It's okay, I'm kind of both," I said with uncertainty. "Names feel complicated these days."

Brand came to my rescue. With a soft chuckle, he asked, "You too?" He placed his hand over his chest and rubbed it in a circle. "Technically my name is Brandon, but ever since the accident I don't feel it. Some days I'm more of a Peter, if that makes sense?"

After a few slow blinks, I was able to focus on Brand. Collin was distracting, but this was important. Very important. "Amnesia?" I asked.

Brand nodded.

"Are your memories more like a history lesson, than a past experience?" I asked.

"Uh, not trauma bonding," Collin complained. "I need another drink."

I was keenly aware as Collin and Bro wandered off. But my attention had been completely captured by Brand's words. Part of me wanted to reach out after Collin, but it was a small part and was instantly drawn back to Brand. Was he like me? This was more important.

"I've regained most of my memory. But at first it was very difficult. It was as if I was two different people in my brain."

"And now?" I may have leaned a little too close. He had something far more interesting going on than his objective physical attractiveness. I was more interested in what was going on in his brain, or whoever's brain it was.

"Now he's Brand," Gil said. "He's got all of his memories. All of them, if you know what I mean?"

My jaw dropped, and I covered my open mouth with my

hands. Had Brand lived a different life before? Maybe I wasn't alone in this.

"You said you were struggling with your name being who you are. Who do you want to be?" Brand asked.

"Not Addison," I said with a shake of my head.

"So, I can still call you Mancey?" Emi asked with a weak giggle.

I sort of nodded and shrugged all at once. "It's who I am. And I don't have Addison's mother here to fight over it. Truthfully, the more I find out about my past, I really don't like who I was. I feel sorry for that woman, and I never want to be her again."

"She talks about herself in the third person like you used to," Gil pointed.

"You know, you can always get your name legally changed to whatever you want," Brand offered.

"Maybe I will. I still haven't switched back to Addison's maiden name after the divorce," I thought out loud. "Maybe I'll have my name changed to something completely different."

6

During the days following Emi's wedding, I didn't know what to do with myself. I was in Hawaii. Everything was gorgeous and hot. And it wasn't as if Collin was just wandering around the neighborhood for me to run into. Not that I was staying in Emi's neighborhood, even if he was.

It was time to accept that if I was going to stay in Hawaii, I needed a plan. Where was I going to live, and what was I going to do? And if I was going to tempt Collin in any way, I also needed a very specific plan for that— since my original hopes of him instantly falling at my feet and declaring his undying love upon our first meeting didn't happen.

Honestly, I screwed up my wedding opportunity epically. I couldn't help it. Brand hadn't exactly said it out loud, but he too had once been someone else. Plan A had been a complete flop. I needed a plan B, one that might actually convince Collin that I was the woman for him.

I didn't know how to do that. But I was pretty certain that getting a sunburn at the beach was not going to be one of the action items. Fortunately, investing in an umbrella was easy enough. I may have looked like a nut job sitting at the beach while hiding under an umbrella, but I didn't want a sunburn, and Addy's skin did not tan.

"Your phone is ringing," Addy pointed out. I hadn't noticed at first. I was lost in that infinite space where the horizon of the ocean and sky merge, trying to figure out what to do with this life I now had.

"It's your mother," I announced before answering. "Hello?"

'Put it on speakerphone. I want to hear Mom.'

"When are you coming home?" Addison's mother immediately asked, whining over the phone.

She was angry with me. Disappointed. Her disappointment was hidden under the guise of just being concerned. After all, Addison was acting so weird. As if *weird* was an insult. Weird was different, and different was the spice of life.

"I don't know if I am coming back, Kristen."

"Mother. Mom. Call me Mom," she corrected.

I took a deep breath and wondered why I had answered the phone, knowing it was her on the other end of the line.

"I think I'm going to stay here for a while," I told her.

"But I don't understand," she practically wailed.

"That's just it, Kristen. You never understand. I can talk until I'm blue in the face. I can explain myself using every word in the dictionary, and you always don't understand."

"You don't have to be so mean, Addison."

'She's right, that was rude.'

I glared at Addy. She had been perfectly willing to let this woman control her life. That was not something I was going to allow.

"I'm not Addison," I said again. "I don't like that name."

"But I gave you that name. Why are you rejecting everything?"

I let out a ragged sigh.

"I'm rejecting everything because that is no longer me." I spoke in short, concise terms, hoping maybe if I simplified my vocabulary, she might actually clue in. "The Addison you knew, the Addison I was, is no longer."

'I'm right here, Mom!' Addy leaned over the phone and yelled.

"You want me to treat you as if you just died that day?"

"You might be better off if you did," I retorted.

"But Addy—"

"Kristen. Mom. I need to find out who I am, and I am not going to be able to do that with you constantly hovering over me."

"But do you have to do it in Hawaii?"

I looked at the surrounding landscape— rich, green, luscious hills at my back, clear sand, and the infinite blue of the ocean and the sky in front of me. If I couldn't find myself here, then this was where I wanted to get lost.

"I'm not going to find myself in Moscow. I keep running into people who think they know me, and I haven't a clue who they are." I wanted to tell her about how it felt being ambushed by Tyler's first wife— a woman who Addison had somehow cheated out of an abusive husband— and I felt bad for her, not for me, because clearly Addison had been in the wrong. But I also felt bad for Addison. She had been a child. A child who didn't understand what her parents had pressured her into. And while I understood that she needed to get out from under their control, her ex-husband's control, and the control of the people who thought they knew better for her, I don't think Addy did.

After talking to Brand, I realized that if Addison's memories were going to come back to me, she needed to want them to. I didn't think that was going to happen while she maintained a separate existence as a ghost. Honestly, I didn't feel the need to integrate my life with hers. The history of this body and the history of me had been two different lives that had somehow coalesced into one going forward.

I had no one I could tell this to. Not even Addy. I had to figure this out on my own. I certainly couldn't tell it to Addison's mother.

"There's a program here," I started. "For adults starting college. I thought I might look into it."

I had started the lie about being a college student when speaking with George O'Connell, and it was an easy one to remember. Might as well use it on Kristen.

"College? But Addison—"

"But nothing," I cut her off. She might have made that choice for Addy, she wasn't going to be making decisions for me.

"You're not the college type."

"What the hell is that supposed to mean?"

"Language!"

"You don't get to insult me and then call me out for using questionable language. That wasn't even colorful. Come on."

"You know you struggled in high school, dear."

"No. I don't know that!" I practically yelled. "I have amnesia, remember?"

I glared at Addy, she certainly hadn't been much help letting me know about her past. Her high school grade point average had never been a topic of conversation.

"Yes, but really—"

"Kristen," I cut her off, "I can't remember anything prior to waking up in the hospital."

"But I told you—"

"I know you've told me, and again, I repeat, I cannot remember anything prior to waking up in the hospital. You're the one acting like you've got amnesia, or maybe it's early onset dementia, because you seem to not remember that I'm the one with memory issues!"

I heard a sob, and then some scrambling noises, and then Bob's voice.

"Now, Addison, you've upset your mother."

'Hi Dad! I'm here!' Addy said as if he could hear her. She sounded so hopeful.

"Bob," I said calmly, "she upset herself."

"When are you coming home, sweetheart?"

"I don't know where home is, and that's what I'm trying to figure out."

'Home is in Idaho, you know that. Can we go home?'

"Your home's with us."

"Is it really? Because the last time I was there, the two of you were trying to convince me that home was with my ex-husband."

"Now, Addison, there's no need to be like that."

"I am an adult. I may not remember my childhood, but I know how to be an adult. And right now, that means I have to do a little self-discovery and get out from under the control— and get away from people— who are trying to control me. I do not want to be a mini version of Kristen. And from everything everybody's told me, I definitely do not want to be the way I had been."

I took a breath.

'Sorry Addy, but I'm not you, I can't be you, or who you

were.' I said to her before returning to the phone conversation.

"I'm staying in Hawaii for right now. I suggest you guys don't try to track me down," I said as I ended the call.

I should have hung up earlier. Everything Kristen wasn't willing to listen to, I had hoped Bob was. After all, he had always seemed the more reasonable of the two parents ever since I regained consciousness in this body.

"Well," I muttered, "looks like I made one decision. I'm staying in Hawaii."

"I hate you. Give me back my life." Addy flickered and then was gone.

I felt an odd buzzing through my body. And then there was a pop, and Addy was back in front of me, glowering like an angry wasp.

I took a deep breath. "You vacated the premises. I don't think you can just jump back in and un-ghost yourself."

"I'm not a ghost! I'm consciousness outside of my body."

"Addison darling, that's the definition of a ghost."

Addy grumbled some more before abandoning me for however long until she decided to come back.

"Might as well see what it would take to be a student," I said to no one.

If I wanted to apply to be a student at University of Hawaii, I was going to need some information. And while I was pretty certain Addison didn't know how to use a library, I was well-versed in how to conduct research.

Once my mind was made up, it was a matter of getting myself to the library during open hours. And once that was achieved, I had to face down modern technology.

I wasn't afraid of technology. However, the last time I got my hands on anything that resembled a computing machine, punch tape had been involved. I didn't really think of the phone as a computer, even though it technically was one.

The computer terminal I sat in front of was all icons and clicks. The interface was child's play. I had missed the early days of modern computing— being non-corporeal and completely uninterested. A typewriter keyboard was the same whether it was on a computer or a typewriter. I just needed to remember what to double-click, when to double-click, and when to right-click.

The World Wide Web was amazing.

I knew my way around a card file. I knew my way around microfiche. I knew how to assess a document for its research value. But with this computer and the internet, I could do it all while sitting on my backside, in one place. No running back and forth between the card catalog and a stern-faced reference librarian. And no dank out-of-the-way stacks with creepy dark rooms to read the films.

With a few clicks of my fingers, I discovered that Dr. Collin Paulo only took graduate-level students and lectured on campus every other semester— neither of which applied to the upcoming semester.

He and his team were doing field research full-time this semester, and only graduate students in the program were accepted to work at the site.

"Damn," I said, clicking through more program details.

If I didn't have any college credit at all, that meant I would have to apply and be accepted as an incoming freshman. I wouldn't be able to get near Collin as a professor for several years, even if I fast-tracked. Maybe this wasn't going to work out.

What good would it do me to be a student on one island when Collin and his research were stationed on another?

This was beginning to feel like being a student wasn't such a good idea.

And probably Collin's integrity was such that he wouldn't even contemplate having an inappropriate relationship with a student while he was a professor.

I sighed.

I bet his classes were full of young women just there to study his geological formations. The man was a hunk. And I was singularly determined for him to be my hunk. I was going to need another plan. Plan C.

I signed out of the computer terminal, as the librarian had instructed— and the step-by-step instructions taped to the side of the desk showed. I pushed my chair back and stood up.

"Did you get the information you needed?" the librarian asked in a hushed, professional voice.

"I think so." I sounded dejected to my own ears.

"Not the answer you were looking for?"

"It was what I was looking for," I said. "But not the answer I wanted, exactly."

"Well, let me know if you need to log back on at any time, okay?"

I thanked her and wandered out of the library. I didn't know where I was going to go or what I was going to do. The whole college idea— well, easy enough for Mancey— just appeared to be impossible for Addison.

That reminded me. I still needed to change my name. Addy had never changed her name after the divorce back to her maiden name. Something I suspected Kristen and Bob had influenced.

I was still legally Addison Jones, and I felt like I was running into her problems. Not mine. Problems that she probably would never see a way out of. Problems that should have barely been a challenge for me. I may not have known what my name needed to be, but I knew the Jones needed to go. I could handle being Addison Mancey Rouche until I figured out exactly who I was.

As I strolled, I noticed what looked like a flea market set up in a parking lot. There were folding tables and, in some spaces, just blankets with random stuff laid out.

I needed the distraction.

'This all looks like Dad's work shed,' Addy said as a means of reintroducing her presence.

I wasn't exactly shopping for anything. Not as if I needed anything. I was currently living in a hotel, trying to figure out what my next move was going to be. I needed to clear my head and stop thinking.

'It does,' I agreed.

As I strolled past tables covered with old knick-knacks, saved from somebody's collection, and a stack of vinyl albums that apparently nobody had players for anymore... I just stopped thinking.

'Look at all this junk,' she complained.

A woman in a traditional Hawaiian print dress smiled and nodded. This rummage sale wasn't like some kind of foreign bazaar where people were constantly shilling their goods. This looked more like families cleaning out their attics— leftover Christmas and Halloween decorations they no longer needed, or a grandma's old figurine collection nobody understood why she liked in the first place, and nobody wanted anymore.

I let my fingers trail a few inches about the stuff, as if I was touching it.

These were the memories of people's lives that were gone. This rummage sale made me think all this stuff belonged to people who were no longer with us. Is this what

Kristen and Bob had to look forward to— getting rid of Addison's stuff? Did Addison have collections and belongings that had meaning to her? Meaning that was lost with her memories?

'You didn't have any collections, did you? I don't remember seeing anything in your room.'

'No, but Mom is going to give me her Christmas Village.'

I tried to look at her. She wasn't fully there, more of a flickering presence with an annoying voice.

'Oh right. I guess she'll be giving it to you now.'

I shook my head. *'Nope, I don't like dust catchers.'*

'Please, you never had any kind of collection? Not even salt and pepper shakers?'

My thoughts were getting entirely too maudlin and depressed. Struggling with who I was, what I knew... looking at people's belongings that had no value anymore just made me want to cry.

'Not even silver spoons. I don't want to end up like this, my prized possessions as someone else's junk.'

I may not have liked who Addison had been. But I was also not liking who Mancey was right now.

'Hey, Mancey, this looks like that radio thing you were messing with back home.'

I moved on to the next table— and caught my breath as I saw what Addy had been looking at. Displayed in front of me were old transistors, copper wires, and vacuum tubes. I recognized radio parts, old soldering irons. Something tickled in the back of my brain. It wasn't a plan, not yet at least.

"How much do you want for all of this?" I asked the teenager on the other side of the table.

He looked at me and shrugged. "It's all old crap. I don't know— make me an offer."

I quickly looked in my bag. His 'old crap' was the technology I was used to.

"Nobody wants this stuff," he added. "I've got some old computer parts here too." He picked up a plastic bucket that was full of green flat boards with black paneling, tiny little resistors on it.

I glanced around to see if I could spot that soldering iron again. I definitely wanted that. I moved the bucket closer to me. I looked around for more wire. I was sure soldering wire hadn't gone out of use. If nothing else, I could buy some new.

I held out a handful of twenties, then drew a circle in the air, indicating everything I wanted.

"Is this enough?"

"Sure, yeah. You need a box?"

He took the money. I started to pull all the items close to me.

"Yes please, a box, or even a bag if you have one?"

Five minutes later, I was heading back in the direction of my hotel. I had a paper sack full of transistors and little glass vacuum tubes, and the tools of the technology I knew.

'What are you going to do with all of that?' Addy asked.

'I'm not one hundred percent sure, but I'm going to do something.'

7

The Jeep rolled to a stop.

"Are you sure this is the right place?" my driver asked.

I looked out the window.

We were on the edge of the Volcanoes National Park. One of those white pavilion party tents was set up in front of a large fifth wheel next to a beat-up pickup truck.

"Yeah, this is it," I said as I climbed out of the back.

My driver scrambled from the car and pulled my wheeled suitcases out of the back. I wrestled my large tote bag onto my shoulder and held my hat firmly down.

Under the party tent, a large shadowy figure sat hunched in front of a laptop.

"Here you go. You sure you don't want me to wait around, make sure all's good?"

"All's good," I said.

This was the mobile research headquarters of UH's Mobile Vulcan Study Lab. I was pretty certain that the shadowy figure behind the computer was exactly who I needed to see.

I reached into my tote bag and found the file folder of documents I needed. I straightened up, then grabbed the handles of my two suitcases. They rolled and bumped awkwardly as I made my way tentatively over the broken ground. I was not dressed appropriately for field work, but I looked good, and that was the point.

The glare of the afternoon sun was just wrong, and I couldn't clearly see into the dark shadows under the tent.

"Hey, can I help you?" the man called out. His voice was grumbly and deep, but it didn't sound familiar.

"Yeah, I'm looking for Dr. Paulo," I said.

"Hey, I remember you," a completely different man said.

Emerging from deep in the shadows was someone I hadn't noticed. Bro, from Emi's wedding, emerged into the light. He wore cargo shorts and a faded old T-shirt.

"Bro?" I asked.

"Yeah, you remember me from Emi's wedding? Addison, right? Wait— no, no. It wasn't that, sorry..."

"Addison, right," I confirmed.

"But that's not right, is it? Emi used a different name for you."

I shook my head and then started nodding. "Right. Addison. But that's not my name anymore. I took some advice and am in the process of getting my name changed. I'm going by Mancey now," I said.

Twisting in my stomach sent all of my nerves on end. It felt good to announce who I was.

"Mancey Rouche. I also took back my maiden name, so Addison Jones officially no longer exists."

"I'm sorry, or congratulations. Which should it be?"

"I think it should be congratulations. This is a good change."

"I didn't realize you worked with Dr. Paulo, right? Are you a graduate student too?" I asked.

"Not me. I'm one of the professors. Dr. Brody Nakamura. What are you doing here? You aren't one of our students?"

"Actually, I am. I'm supposed to check in with Dr. Paulo." I held out the top sheet of paper from my file.

Bro looked at it. "Hey, Collin, you're going to want to see this."

The shadowy figure under the tent stood. Damn, Collin was huge. Collin reached past Bro and snatched the paper from me. He grumbled as he read over the letter of introduction.

"What's this?" He waved the paper at me.

His voice was low and all hard, round edges, like a rock. It wasn't soft in any way. It was older, sturdy, and strong. He was dressed similarly to Bro in cargo shorts, faded shirt, and little plastic flip-flops. I wondered if he should have been wearing more sturdy footwear, especially working around lava.

"Hi. Hello again. Nice to see you. I don't know if you remember me from your sister's wedding."

"Yeah, I remember you," he said. "What can I help you with?"

I handed him the rest of the file of papers. He took them from my hands and began leafing through them.

"You should have received information about me. I was told you'd be expecting me. You should have received a letter, more specifically an email."

Collin looked up at me, confused.

"I'm a visiting student on a research grant from the University of Idaho. I do related geological research. It's all in the documents there. I've developed a hypothesis regarding tectonic plate movement."

I stumbled over my words. I had practiced this. I was a movie star. I should be able to convince these men that I was a student with a strong hypothesis in tectonic plate theory. Yet, I was nervous. I was completely blowing this audition.

Bro looked over Collin's shoulder at the top letter. "Communications?" he asked.

I nodded. This was ridiculous. I shouldn't have been scared. If they didn't buy my story, how was I ever going to convince Collin to pay attention to me?

"And how does that place you at my field research camp?" Collin asked.

I swallowed. A lump sat heavy in my throat.

"I believe there are electric pulse signals that—" I braced my mental loins and began my pitch again. "I believe there are electric pulse signals that are released like a form of announcing plate movement."

"You're talking about the ground announcing it's going to move? Like for an earthquake?"

"In the simplest of terms— precisely. But more like how lightning precedes a thunderclap."

"And since tectonic plate movement is so unpredictable and slow... I'm out here on a grant to work alongside active volcanoes to see if they're sending out signals in a similar fashion."

"Huh," was all he said. "Well, you do get lightning strikes with volcanic eruptions..."

He continued to flip through the pages in my folder.

"Hey. Yeah, what's up?" A woman called out from the other side of the tent.

I glanced up as she walked toward us.

She was about my height. Her dark hair was pulled back into a thick braid. She wore a crocheted crop-top sweater with bell sleeves and high-waisted short shorts. Her thighs were intimidating, and she walked with the kind of confidence Addison had never possessed. She had extra curves— not unlike myself— but moved with absolute strength.

My body was a marshmallow compared to her, soft in its shape, light in coloring.

"We have a new grad student. Mancey, Leia. Leia, Mancey," Collin introduced us.

"Hi," I offered, holding out my hand.

Her grip was firm. I was right— she radiated strength.

Her face had been hidden behind aviator sunglasses and a ball cap. She pulled off her cap, wiped sweat from her brow, and removed the sunglasses. Strong. Intimidatingly beautiful. Perfect. Exactly what I needed to be dealing with — competition.

It wasn't enough that I was going to have to compete for Collin's attention against an active volcano. Now, I had to deal with her.

Maybe she was Bro's girlfriend? Maybe she wasn't even interested in Collin.

She gave me one of those raking glances— down to my feet, lingering at my inappropriate footwear, and then back up to my inappropriate clothing.

I smiled, letting her know that what she had just done to me had not gone unnoticed. After all, I had probably done the same assessment to her. I attempted to adjust my expression— hopefully, so I didn't mirror the same sneer I saw on her face.

"I guess the guys will be glad there's one more of us," she added.

"She's not exactly one of us," Collin said.

"What do you mean?"

"She has her own research." He handed the file folder

back to me. "She's here to basically work alongside us— see if she can coordinate her findings with our findings."

"Huh," Leia said.

She stepped behind the make shift desk and opened a cooler I hadn't noticed earlier. She took out a tall thermos, unscrewed the cap, drank something, recapped it, then put it back in the cooler.

I guessed working on a lava flow was hot work.

She settled her ball cap back on her head and returned to wherever she had come from.

I was the only one who watched her walk away, which was a shame. The men really should have been admiring the sway of her hips. She certainly wasn't walking that way for me.

"Where are you staying?" Bro asked.

"Well, I thought I was going to be staying with your team," I said.

I glanced toward the fifth wheel, but there was no way more than four full-grown adults were going to fit in there comfortably.

"We've got a rental cabin for the students, but there's no additional room for you," Collin announced.

"Oh," I murmured. "I have a housing allowance with my grant. I guess that means I'm on my own."

I looked down, trying to hide the disappointment. *Shit.* I hadn't planned on being separated from them. I thought they'd be camping. Not that I liked camping, but I was willing to do what it took.

I bit my lip, thinking.

"I guess I can see if there are any short-term rentals. You wouldn't happen to know of any places nearby, would you?"

"No," Collin answered.

"Did I overhear you talk about finding a place to stay?" A

slender woman stepped out from the fifth wheel. She looked at Collin questioningly.

He nodded at me.

"It looks like I need a place to stay so that I can be present to conduct my research," I explained.

"There's a campground not too far," she offered. "They might have cabins. You can check them out."

"Oh. Okay. Can I at least leave my equipment here?"

My plan felt like it was circling the drain before it could even take shape.

"Yeah, we can find space in the lab," Collin said.

I looked up at the camper.

"Oh... you're not staying in there?"

"No, that's our on-site lab," he replied. "You can put your stuff in there. For now."

No one offered to pick up either of my bags. Only one of them was full of equipment, but still. The new woman held the door open for me while I wrestled it up the awkward, narrow stairs into the RV.

"I'm Sadie. Are you another grad student?"

"Everyone here is a grad student," Bro rumbled behind me.

"Kind of. Only, I'm not a geology student. I'm researching communications."

Inside, it looked exactly as I expected an RV trailer to look. Only instead of a bedroom, there were folding tables, desks with laptops set up.

I needed to make a few adjustments to my plan— especially if I wanted to be taken seriously.

"I guess you can use that desk," Sadie said, pointing to one of the unoccupied tables.

"Thanks." I lifted the suitcase and began unpacking. I had stacks of notebooks, pens, pencils, and a few contraptions I was going to use to track the communication signals I claimed to be interested in.

I didn't have a computer. That was definitely going to have to change— especially if I wanted them to buy my story that I was a research student. I was planning to take notes and run calculations the old-fashioned way, with pencil and paper. I even had a slide rule with me.

When I stepped out of the fifth wheel, I noticed my other suitcase— the one I had left near the white party tent — was gone.

Collin sat in the driver's seat of the pickup truck and waved at me. "I got your stuff. Come on, I'll take you over to the campground. We can see if they've got a place for you. You don't have a car, do you?"

I shook my head.

"Well, maybe you can get a—"

I shook my head again. "I didn't think I was going to need one," I said reluctantly as I climbed in and sat next to him. My nerves did a happy dance sitting next to Collin.

"It's not too far, but I don't think you're going to want to walk every day. You might want to think about getting a bike."

"Okay," I nodded. I added bicycle to my mental shopping list, right under laptop computer.

"Hold on!" Bro jumped into the back, and slapped the side of the truck twice.

When we got to the campgrounds, I fumbled with my seat belt and climbed out of the cab of the truck, smoothing my skirt down. This outfit had been calculated to gain maximum male gaze, and from the smirk that danced across Bro's lips, it was working. But it was working on the wrong man.

Collin barely glanced at me as he pulled my bag from the back of the truck.

I took my time climbing the stairs. Maybe he would catch the wiggle in my steps this time.

Bro crashed in past me, and before I even made it to the top of the stairs he leaned out, beckoning for me to come on in.

"I guess I need to see if you have any cabins I can stay in," I announced.

"We've got a single, but how long do you want it for?" the young man asked. He couldn't have been more than a teenager.

I raised my eyes questioningly as I turned to Bro.

"I'm supposed to be attached to your group. How long are they planning on being in the field?"

"We're usually out for six weeks at a time, but if something exciting happens, we might stay longer," Bro answered.

I turned to the young man at the counter, he looked at me like I was some weirdo asking him questions he didn't know. I hitched my thumb to point at Bro. "I guess six weeks, with an option to extend," I grimaced as I spoke.

The young man typed away on what looked like the screen of a computer, but I didn't see where the keyboard was hidden. I leaned over and watched him work.

"Is that one of those tablets?" I asked.

He must have thought I was a nut, the way I used old people language asking about the tech he was using.

"Wouldn't a computer be easier?"

"Nah, man." He wiggled the tablet. "This thing is bigger than the last laptop we used. More power, and I can take it with me when I'm checking the grounds. I can make my notes straight into this."

I looked at Bro. "Do you use one of those?"

He shrugged. "Sometimes."

"But didn't I see you working on a laptop earlier?"

"We have multiple ways of tracking data into the database," he said. Bro gestured to the tablet the young man was working on. "His might be more powerful. The ones we have don't have that much RAM."

RAM. I tucked that away into the back of my head as a reminder to look up more computer lingo.

"But the tablets we can heat shield better, so they'll go out onto the lava flows with us."

"Interesting." I chewed on my lip again while I waited for the kid to finally look up from his work.

"Okay, you're gonna have to move twice, but I can keep you in a cabin for six weeks with an extension."

"Why can't she just stay in one cabin?" Bro asked.

"Do I have to move?"

"People reserve specific cabins. I don't know. They're all the same to me, man."

"I can move twice. I don't have that much stuff with me."

"Okay, here's your key." He slid an old-fashioned key on a plastic hotel fob across the desk at me.

Little did I realize that that was the easy part.

"And this is the code to the bathhouse." He wrote and then circled four numbers on a large printout. "And this is the Wi-Fi." Then he circled something that was pre-printed on the map.

I let my fingernail drop onto the Wi-Fi password and tapped it a couple of times. That wasn't going to do me any good until I got myself a laptop.

Or maybe... "Where could I get one of those?" I pointed at his tablet.

He shrugged. "There's got to be some places in Hilo you can get it from. Or you could just order what you want."

That gave me an idea. "Can I get deliveries here?" I asked. "I mean, I am going to be staying here for a while."

He shrugged again. "Of course, yeah. Just have them send it to the office. We have people do that all the time."

I looked at Bro, and then I looked at the young man.

"Do you think you could help me order one of those tablets? And maybe a bicycle? I'm going to need some bedding too."

I chewed on the tip of my fingernail as the young man looked confused and Bro broke out into a broad smile.

8

It only took my tablet twenty-four hours to arrive. It took longer for the bike.

Mark— the kid behind the counter— was some kind of tablet genius. Not only did I have a top-of-the-line tablet with extra memory and extra RAM— which I learned meant computing power— but he made sure I had the applications I needed. He also made sure I had an impact-resistant, heat-shielded case, and he created an account in the cloud for me. That meant a secure computer located somewhere else in the world for backing up all of my data, so I could retrieve it from any computer anywhere, as long as I had my passwords.

Mark was now my new best friend.

Learning to use the tablet felt more like playing than anything else. Mark showed me all the best free training videos and recommended his favorite video games.

It made me giggle every time Bro caught me playing a video game, or drawing in ProCreate, he would grumble. He's the one who recommended a tablet after Mark showed off the one he was using.

Until my bicycle bothered to arrive, I was stuck walking.

"Hey, it's getting late," Clark announced, as we all sat hunched over our makeshift desks, reviewing the data everyone had collected on their assorted projects.

I hadn't quite mastered the calculations program yet, and I was transcribing all of my data back and forth from my tablet into my notebook, and the other way round, so that I could run calculations by hand.

Leia looked up. "Oh yeah, look at that. It's dark. When did that happen?"

It hadn't been dark when I'd taken a break for dinner. I didn't know if anybody else had bothered to eat that evening. It was late enough that I knew I shouldn't walk. It was dark, and there were no sidewalks and limited light. I was going to have to beg a ride off Collin or one of the other students. Or I could suck it up and call an Uber.

"Well, I'm gonna clock out for the day and turn in," Collin announced. "Don't stay too late."

"Yeah, see ya," Bro muttered.

It was such an odd phrase for Collin to say, we didn't have a time clock, we worked to the work. Which meant we were always working. I was deep into my calculations, and it was several minutes before I realized what he had said.

Crap.

If I was going to be able to get a ride home from him, I needed to have left five minutes earlier. But I wasn't done. I would just have to finish this back at my cabin. I quickly gathered my notebooks, tablet, and pencils, and shoved them into the messenger bag I used to carry everything I needed back and forth between the cabin and the lab.

I ran out the door completely oblivious to my manners, not saying goodbye— even though Leia, at most, would just grunt at me. To say Leia and I hadn't bonded would have been an understatement. It wasn't that we didn't get along, but we were definitely not friends. But Sadie, Clark, and Bro all deserved a farewell.

The RV door banged shut behind me just as I watched the taillights of Collin's truck disappear around the corner.

"Damn it," I spit out.

I had missed my chance of getting a ride with him. I looked around the site. The only car left was Leia's. I stared at it for a long while. I could either go back inside and throw myself at her feet and beg for mercy, or I could walk.

I really had to think about it. Exactly how hard was it going to be to go ask Leia for a ride? The grad students were all staying at a long-term rental that was in the other direction from the campgrounds.

"I thought you left," Sadie asked as I stepped inside.

"I tried. But I missed my chance at asking Collin for a ride."

"Dr. Paulo," Leia corrected. "You really shouldn't call him by his first name. He's your research advisor, not your friend."

"He's your research advisor, not mine. And I met him..." I paused, she didn't need to know my business. "I know his sister. I met him outside of the academic setting."

With a huff, I turned to drop my messenger bag on my desk and pull out my phone. "I guess I'm calling a car."

"Or I could walk you back," Bro said. He stood and leveled me with a heated gaze.

I felt tingles I didn't want to acknowledge.

"Or I could walk," I said. I needed the fresh air to cool me down a notch. I was projecting onto Bro. He was attractive with high broad cheek bones and warm brown eyes. But I was after Collin, and I didn't need the distraction of another overtly handsome man.

I hiked my bag back on my shoulder. "Bye, again," I said as I stepped outside this time.

Bro followed, letting the screen door bang close behind him. He shoved his hands in his pockets and followed along next to me. "You have to walk this every day?"

"Not every day. I've grabbed a couple of rides from the other students."

"Leia gave you a ride?"

I laughed. I guess it was pretty obvious the two of us did not get along. "No, not Leia. But Sadie and Clark have when she wasn't around. The kid from the campground has been really great about giving me rides in the morning. I buy him breakfast and pay for gas, and he runs me up on his scooter."

"You could always take an Uber."

I snorted. "It would be cheaper to buy a car for how expensive Uber is around here. I guess there just aren't that many drivers. Honestly, with tourism, I thought there would be more."

I watched his face as lights bounced across his features. He was probably better looking than Collin. And Collin was gorgeous. Bro's mouth was particularly tempting. Especially when he smiled.

Bro's hands and arms kept moving as if they were swaying through water. He didn't leave them hanging at his side. He was always moving, even when everyone was standing around looking at readout displays on the various computers everyone worked on.

"You're always doing that." I pointed to the movements. "I've seen Collin do it too. Are you channeling the lava or something?"

Bro barked out a laugh. "Channeling lava, as if." He repeated the actions, only this time he used his full range of motion. He slapped his hands against his thighs a few times, and twisted around, incorporating some foot work.

"Oh." I figured it out. "You're a kāne dancer like Collin, aren't you?"

"You know Collin is a dancer?"

I nodded. "Remember, friends with his sister. She took me to a performance once."

"Well then, you've seen me too. We're in the same dance group."

I couldn't remember ever seeing Bro perform, but now that I knew, of course he was a dancer. It was so obvious, he moved like one, and I didn't just mean the running through a routine in his head part. He had grace, and strength. Now I knew what he could do, I really wanted to see him move. I really wanted to see him in his stage outfit with all his skin exposed. Would he be as captivating as Collin?

"You know, what you said back there, you were technically wrong."

"About what? Your dancing? Are you walking me back to my cabin so you can scold me?" My words were sharper than my tone. I was mostly teasing him. I appreciated the company, it made the few miles go by faster.

"Collin," Bro started.

I sucked in a breath. Did he know I was playing compare and contrast with his and Collin's smiles? Did he know I had images of him in performance garb spinning in my head? I gulped and made a non-committal sound in my throat.

"He is your advisor. All that documentation you brought with you clearly puts you under his academic guidance."

"So you don't think I should call him Collin either?"

"Of course you should call him that. It's his name," Bro chuckled.

"So, what's your point?" I asked.

"My point is..." Bro stopped walking.

I stopped and turned to face him.

A slow smile tugged at his lips until his teeth gleamed at me. He stepped in close and ran his hand down my arm from shoulder to elbow. His fingers felt like the tickle of a static charge. He held me in place and inched in closer.

A shiver skittered along my spine. My body responded with flutters and tightening of sensitive bits all on its own.

His eyes dropped to my lips. "The point is, Mancey, I'm not your advisor."

His gaze returned to my eyes, and it was my turn to keep looking at his mouth. I licked my lower lip before sucking it in between my teeth. I may have moved in even closer. There was palpable energy surging between us.

The bright lights and blaring horn from a car broke the tension. Bro swung me around and farther off the pavement.

My heart thudded in my throat. I couldn't be sure if it was from the scare of the loud and entirely too close car, or from the closeness of Bro.

He kept his distance the rest of the walk to the campground.

When we arrived at my cabin, my new bike was parked in front of my door. A note tied to the handle bars indicated the keys were in the office.

"I guess I no longer need to walk," I said as I checked it out.

"A tricycle? Are you three? You need a helmet," Bro said as he looked it over.

The bike was a lovely soft teal color with a wide basket between the back wheels.

"I already have a helmet. It showed up right away. I'm not sure why, but getting the bike here took forever. And yes, a tricycle. It's electric, and the basket is big enough for shopping."

"It looks pretty fancy. You might want to lock it up in your cabin at night," Bro suggested as he knelt down and examined the battery pack.

"It needs a key to run. No one can ride off with it."

"They don't have to ride away with it, they can toss it in the back of a truck." Bro mimicked a lifting motion.

"Or just walk away with it in their arms," I said with a sigh as I realized how easy it had to be for someone with Bro's strength to pick it up. "I can't keep it inside. It will take up all the room."

"It should be safe at the lab site during the day, but I wouldn't trust your camping neighbors. If you won't keep it inside, at least get a good bike lock, one that can't easily be cut off."

He offered suggestions as I wrestled it inside my cabin for the night, but no real help otherwise. I'd order a lock and chain as soon as I had a minute.

"Thanks for your help," I said sarcastically as I leaned against the door.

Bro stood on the verge of stepping off the small covered patio.

"Did you walk me home just so you could let me know you're not my advisor?" I chewed on my bottom lip. Collin may have been my end game, but I could be convinced into changing objectives.

He gave me that slow easy grin exposing a glint of white teeth. His voice was low in both timbre and tone. It made my toes and other bits curl and tingle. I could definitely change my objectives.

"That's exactly why I walked you home." He turned and

skipped off the step. He shoved his hands into his pockets, squared up his shoulders and sauntered away.

I watched his dancer-firm back side until he turned the corner around the front office. Squealing like a teenager, I kicked off my shoes before jumping onto my bed. There was something thrilling in knowing he had his eye on me. The flirting with George O'Connell had been one thing, but this felt different. This was different, and I couldn't put my finger on it.

I stayed up way too late running calculations. In the morning, I discovered that apparently Addison had not only not known how to swim, but apparently she didn't know how to ride a bike either. I was glad I got the tricycle. Even with the stability of three wheels, I still managed to fall off.

I arrived at the lab with a skinned knee and a little shaken up over the wobbly ride. The RV was empty, I figured everyone had gone over to the lava flows and were collecting data there.

I wanted to run my calculations a second time. My little recording device seemed to actually be collecting real information. My hypothesis had really been nothing more than a ploy to get into the company of Collin, but the data...

"This is so boring," Addy exclaimed as she appeared out of nowhere.

She poked at the print-outs on Sadie's desk before moving to the other desks in the room.

"Is that why you've been M.I.A?"

"M.I.A? Mia? What are you even talking about? You know my name is Addy." She snorted out her question as if I was the one being dumb.

"Missing in action, Addison. You haven't been around much," I said.

"All of this is so boring. You're studying for fun. Ew."

"I'm collecting data to support my thesis," I told her.

"I don't know what that means." She flopped to the best of her ghostly ability on the dinette set. She leaned over, bending double at the waist, and looked down the length of the camper until we made eye contact.

With a huff, I pushed out of my chair and stepped up to where she sat. I slid onto the opposite bench.

"I'm trying to figure something out. So I'm collecting information, and then doing some complicated math to see if the information I have proves an idea I had," I explained.

"Oh. It still sounds boring. How long are you going to keep doing this? I thought we were going to do fun stuff when you came back to Hawaii," she whined like a belligerent teen.

"I'm here to work, not take a vacation."

"I bet you haven't even been to the beach once on this island."

"With this skin?" I held out my hands, showing off the super paleness that was not compatible with the sun. But my arms were a touch pink. "Damn it. Sunburns hurt, and I don't want skin cancer."

"Let me know if you decide to do something fun." She stood, and walked out the door. If she had been corporeal, she would have crashed into Sadie coming into the camper.

Sadie came in with her arms full of equipment, followed by Clark, who seemed to have extra equipment in his arms.

"I didn't expect to see you today," Leia smirked as she came in last.

"What happened to you?" Sadie asked as she looked at me.

"I rode my bike," I said proudly.

"You forgot sunscreen, didn't you?"

I grumbled as I examined the pink developing on my

arms. "Forgot my sunscreen and I fell off the bike a couple of times."

"Here are the keys," Leia said as she reached in her pocket and handed a key ring to Clark, as Sadie and I chatted about my bike.

"Anything else?" he asked.

"We'll be back in a couple of days. Wish us luck." Leis announced as she turned and skipped out of the camper.

"Where is she going?" I asked.

Clark put the collection of laptops and tablets from his arms down on the nearest table. "Some dance competition."

"Leia dances? I knew Collin did, but..."

"Yeah, Dr. Paulo is in some kind of dance troupe. And Leia is a championship soloist," Sadie said.

"Have you seen them perform?" I asked. I was dying to watch Collin dance again.

"Leia, but only when she's messing around," Sadie admitted.

"We should go see them, support them." I suggested.

"We can't. It's during the day, and we are supposed to be working," Clark pointed out.

"It's not like they are going to see us in the audience," I pointed out. "We can work late today, I'll help out. No one cares if I fall a day behind. We should go. And after they dance, we can come right back here."

I had to get Clark on my side and agree to go, after all, he had the car keys, and was going to be my ride.

"Come on, Clark, we should go. It would be fun." Sadie was on my side.

9

———————

It felt like we were sneaking in as Clark, Sadie, and I found seats in the auditorium. We were late, the competition had already started.

"If we get seats back far enough, they won't be able to see us from the stage." I repeated what I remembered from attending an event like this with Emi. She wasn't allowed to sit close to where the dancers could see her because apparently as a kid, she would make faces at Collin and distract other dancers.

"I hope we haven't missed them," I said as I wedged myself into what felt like obnoxiously narrow seats. My hips were going to be bruised.

Sadie handed me a folded program. I began scanning the names. I couldn't tell who was currently performing, but it looked like we hadn't missed who we came to see.

The current dance group finished and left the stage, but the group standing behind a row of drums stayed. The announcer introduced a solo performance.

A woman with long flowing hair made her way onto the stage. She had a wreath of large green leaves and her dress was rather plain compared to what I was expecting. I sat in complete awe as the drums picked up and she began moving. She combined the most graceful flowing arm motions, only to emphasize certain sharp hip motions.

Something deep in my chest tightened. I wanted to be able to dance like her so much. I wanted to look like that instead of what I looked like. I sat there and felt sorry for myself. This was not the afterlife I had wanted when I was floating around eavesdropping on Emi's life.

Sadie grabbed my arm and shook it. "Look, there's Dr. Paulo, I bet his dance group is next."

I focused where she was pointing. I smiled as I saw Collin. Light bounced off his skin in sparkling flashes. I sucked in my breath. Was he sparkling and shiny again?

He had refracted light like he had faceted diamond skin the first time I met him. The light bouncing off him had diminished after I found myself in this body. But maybe it was back?

The soloist finished her performance, and then Collin and Bro's kāne troupe was introduced and made its way to the stage.

Collin twinkled as he took up his position as the second man on stage. Bro was farther back in the line-up, but he also sparkled, as did the rest of the men. It wasn't the light that I had seen coming from him before, it was a lot of body glitter and high-powered stage lights. Even knowing the source of the shimmer, my breath still caught in my throat as the troupe of broad shouldered men took to the stage.

They were glorious. I forgot just how much skin they exposed, and I wanted to touch it all. Collin's tattoo was bigger. It now covered him from wrist to shoulder, crossed his chest, and upper back and down the opposite arm not quite to his elbow. He also had some new markings on his legs, but only from hip to mid-thigh. That tattoo had been completely covered under the cargo shorts he typically wore. I know I hadn't caught a glimpse of it before.

They started with something less aggressive than what I remembered watching with Emi so long ago. The rhythm of the drums started, and the men's lines merged and parted as they stepped into different formations. One group would have their arms lifted, showing off bulging muscles, while their counterparts gestured to the ground. They stepped and twisted, pointing one leg forward, and then the other. And then the two lines merged, and parted again. This time, the first group was acknowledging the earth— I assumed that's what the gesture meant— while the other men lifted their focus to the skies.

It was graceful and almost delicate in their reverence.

I lost track of Collin, even with his distinctive tattoo. And found my gaze constantly being drawn to a different man in the dance troupe, the one with the tattoo that circled below his neck like a wide collar necklace, the one with long wavy hair pulled back, away from his face.

Sadie leaned in against my shoulder. "It feels almost wrong seeing Dr. Paulo without any clothes on."

"He has plenty of clothes on," I laughed.

"He's far too exposed. I'm never going to be able to look him in the eyes again."

"Then focus on any of the other men," I said. Personally, I found focusing on Collin difficult because my gaze kept getting dragged back to Bro. There was simply something about the way Bro moved. I had to force my attention back to Collin. He was supposed to be my goal, not just any Hawaiian dancer man. But Bro wasn't just any man.

I was drawn in by the performance. The men were all fantastic. I could easily swoon at any of their feet. Before I knew it, they were leaving the stage. I scanned the throng to see Collin. My eyes found Bro first, and then I found Collin slightly off to the side. It looked like he was saying something to a woman.

Leia was introduced next, and the woman Collin had been speaking to stepped on to the stage.

My initial thoughts were not kind. I didn't want to be nice about it. If I had thought I wanted to be like the first woman dancer I saw, I was wrong. I wanted to be Leia. Everything about her was perfect. And I was angry about it.

Her skills as a dancer out stripped her physical beauty, and she was stunning, absolutely gorgeous. Her dancing left me speechless. My approach at the remote lab had been all wrong. I shouldn't have been chasing after Collin's approval, but hers. She was strong and fierce, and I should have tried harder to become friends with her.

I watched her leave the stage. Bro was grinning widely at her. I couldn't miss his grin even from where I sat. He patted her shoulder as she stepped past him. And then she was face to face with Collin. They just seemed to stand there and stare at each other in awkward silence. I had no idea if words were exchanged, I was too far away to tell, but their body language was rigid and jerky, the opposite of how either of them had moved while on stage. It looked like he had wanted to hug her, or maybe she was the one who had lurched like a hug had been cut off before it could have begun.

"Okay, that was interesting. But we need to get back," Clark announced.

He rushed us out of the auditorium. I would have liked to stay and watch more dancers. But we had agreed to leave after their performances so that Clark and Sadie wouldn't fall too far behind in their work while their colleagues were away at the dance competition.

Sadie gushed about the performances on the way back. Which was good, because I didn't feel like talking. I kept thinking about how much Leia was living the life I had wanted. I was irrational, as if she had taken something from me. Logically, I knew that wasn't the case. Leia had never taken anything from me. I was the one who had swept in and taken over Addison's life. I was the asshole here.

Leia's dancing had brought tears to my eyes. I didn't hate her, I wanted to be her.

"How hard do you think hula is?" I asked. Maybe if I was a dancer, Collin would pay attention to me. He certainly didn't seem to care about scientific me.

"I tried it once. I thought I was in pretty good shape. I hike, but damn, my thighs were killing me," Sadie said.

"But they make it look so easy," I said.

"That's because they train like crazy," Clark added. "Of course it looks easy, they know what they are doing. You make math look easy."

"Math is easy," I answered.

"Not the way you run calculations," Clark retorted. "I've even seen you use a slide ruler, don't start with me saying that math is easy."

"Don't tell me you never learned to use a slide rule," I said.

"Nobody uses slide rulers, just like no one uses an abacus anymore," Sadie said, practically laughing.

"Well, I learned to use both. But the slide rule is a much better tool for what I'm doing. There are times I think an abacus would be useful, especially when running a tally. So much easier to shuffle beads back and forth than making tick marks, and having to go back and count your marks."

"I think you're crazy. I can do all of that on a computer. Where did you learn all that, anyway? Your equipment looks so steampunk."

Steampunk? Another term to tuck away and look up later.

"I learned a lot of it from my father. He didn't let not having a son stop him from passing on the basics of engineering." Meaning, my actual father. I was pretty sure that Bob, Addison's father, wouldn't know how to use a slide rule either.

10

———

I frenetically sketched in my notebook. I had stacks of them. One waiting to be used, and a second one full of calculations and number crunching.

"You have a top of the line tablet, and you're drawing with a pencil, in a lined notebook?" Bro teased as he propped himself against the table that was my desk, my center of operations.

"Mark has been showing me how to use a drawing program, but I'm still faster with a pencil," I admitted.

As I spoke, he poked at my GeoTalker, that's what I started calling the device I had built. He prodded a tube that functioned as housing for a mess of wires. The tubing was slightly melted. A collection of vacuum tubes and coils of more wires with a couple of signal lights, the GeoTalker was a mishmash of early twentieth century engineering with modern parts. I had used what I could from that fortuitous flea market find, and anything else I could get my hands on.

"Is this a radio?"

"There are some radio parts. After all, I have to narrow in on frequencies to find the signals."

The pine wood frame— more like a housing cage— was sanded smooth, but I hadn't had the inclination to stain the wood. Overall, it was the size of a hefty cat, and it was now showing signs of heat damage with several scorched areas.

"And are you finding signals?" His brow lifted as he shifted his gaze from the device to me.

I glanced at him quickly and had to fight a grin. He had one brow up, it was hot. He was ridiculously cute and smart and made it hard for me to concentrate. I quickly looked away before I combusted from a blush into flames.

"I am." I really hoped he thought my giddiness was because I was having success and not his presence. Maybe it was a little of both, though it heavily leaned toward him.

"What are you drawing up?" Bro asked, his attention back on the GeoTalker as he twisted back and forth, changing his angle to look at it.

I appreciated how he didn't just reach out and touch my little invention. His hands were just in my peripheral vision. They were large and strong, appearing to be perfectly capable. His knees were also in my periphery, but I was choosing to ignore them. They were nice knees, and it took a certain amount of will power to not ogle them.

Besides, I didn't want to ogle Bro. It's not that he wasn't worth a good long gander, he wasn't Collin. Only, Collin wasn't the one who came to see what I was working on. Collin never made comments about me using a pencil instead of the tablet I spent a pretty penny on. I thought for certain Collin would have been the one interested in communicating with lava. But Bro was the one who came and leaned on my desk and showed off his knees.

To be fair, no one was showing off their knees. Just outside the heat suits, everyone tended toward wearing shorts. Myself included. Only, I was showing off my knees in a deliberate attempt to gain a certain someone's attention. I no longer knew why I bothered.

Actually, I did. I was doing it to see which one of these gorgeous men I caught first. It looked like Bro was firmly in my nets. Yet, I still somehow kept trying to convince myself that I had landed the wrong man.

"I'm trying to figure out how I can fabricate a fiber glass box. I don't have any of my tools from back in my old lab."

In the days following the dance showcase, I became distracted by every interaction I witnessed between Leia and Collin. And I put myself in a position just so that I could watch them. As long as they had a common topic— volcanic activity— to discuss, they seemed like any professor student interaction. Any other time, they were awkward around each other. Like they wanted to talk but didn't know how to. There was also this sad longing in their eyes. I think I was the only one to see it. It made my stomach hurt. I wanted that look for me. I wanted Collin in my nets, and it looked like Leia had him.

I drowned my sorrows in my work. I had let the love of science, discovery, and data collection become all encompassing. As long as I had work to do, and data to analyze, I didn't miss Collin nearly so much. And I had data! I had data, and I had Bro. My priorities just needed to catch up.

My little GeoTalker was actually collecting information. I designed and built it mostly for looks. But the science engineer in me didn't let me play pretend. I may have made up the theory simply to get closer to Collin, but if I was going to track tectonic sound frequencies, then I should at least try.

"Why do you need a fiber glass box?" Bro asked.

"Don't touch those." I swatted his hand away from putting his fingers on my vacuum tubes. "I need a heat shield." I pointed to the scorched areas of the wood and the melted plastic tubing.

"But fiber glass? Why not just do what we do?"

I squinted up at him. After I realized my GeoTalker was collecting usable data, other than mooning after Collin, I really hadn't paid much attention to anything the other group was doing. I got copies of their data to correlate with mine, but the actual tools and ways they collected their information was beyond me. They wore silver thermal suits from time to time, but mostly they sat on the side lines and typed away on laptops.

I shook my head. "What?"

"We keep the equipment in coolers."

"Ice would be bad for my device," I tried to point out.

"No ice," Bro chuckled. I was not going to admit that I liked the way laughter rumbled around in his chest. He laughed and rumbled a lot, more than Collin. I couldn't remember a time Collin had laughed since I had arrived. "We double up double walled coolers. Put a heat sink between the layers, and use a solar power supply to keep the fan running. And when the outer shell gets a bit too toasty and melts, we swap it out."

"That explains why there are so many coolers here."

"Yeah, not the best choice, but the most economical and easiest to replace. We make sure they get properly recycled."

"I could probably use some of your discards. I'm not getting nearly as close and friendly to the flows as you are." A bright smile took over my face. I couldn't have stopped it if I had wanted to. I could definitely say this giddy was science related. "You just saved me hours and hours, and lordy knows how much money."

His lips twitched up at the corners. "I'm happy to save you at any time." And then he gave me a broad smile. The corners of his eyes creased up ever so slightly, and I swear they twinkled.

I felt that grin down to my toes. For some reason, a vision of him in his dance garb entered my mind. All of his warm, dark skin, and that neck piece tattoo were what I saw. My internal temperature skyrocketed. I needed one of those heat sinks for my personal components.

The camper's door slammed open and Clark bounded in. "You have got to see this!"

Bro's attention shifted away, breaking whatever spell had just been cast over us. I shuddered, and gave him a few seconds to step away before I tried to get to my feet. I didn't need anyone looking at me while I felt completely unstable.

"No way, man!" Bro said loudly as he looked at whatever Clark had brought in.

"I remember those," Leia said as she glanced over his shoulder.

"What is it?" I asked.

"An old local comic," Leia said.

Clark held up a single panel comic. It showed a little Hawaiian boy in traditional garb holding a large palm frond over…

"Is that supposed to be a wave or lava?" I asked.

The boy in the comic was protecting what looked like a hooked wave shaped rock from the rain. Since the drawing was in black and white, I didn't have the proper context.

"The title says Pele and Pete." I pronounced it as peel and Pete, giving the E-consonant-E similar sounds, making them rhyme.

"It's called Pele and Pete, of course it's lava," Leia said. She pronounced it peh-ley. And her tone wasn't kind.

That was a stupid move. I had only ever heard Pele spoken without seeing it written to make the connection. I was in Hawaii, trying to gain the attention of a volcano specialist, and I had just fumbled massively on the name of what was essentially his patron goddess. If I was going to be thought of as dumb, I could either lean in, or pretend it didn't happen. I knew how I felt about people who tried to pretend their dumb wasn't out there.

"Well, don't I look foolish. I don't think I've ever knowingly seen Pele's name written out before. Pele and Pete, that's cute. A little boy and his pet lava?" I asked.

A low, throaty chuckle started in Bro's throat. "You know who this is, right?"

"That's supposed to be Dr. Paulo," Clark answered.

"No way," Leia said indignantly. "That's not Dr. Paulo."

"It is," Bro admitted. "Our very own Collin Paulo has been playing with lava for a very long time. A family friend saw him out at the park with his family and got the idea."

"I know, right? Dr. Paulo was a kid once." Clark laughed

The camper door swung open with a loud crash. Someone really needed to do something about the crappy hinges on that thing.

Collin stepped inside. "What are you doing? I'm out there waiting. Come on."

"Sure thing, Pete," Bro said with a snicker under his breath.

"You mustn't keep Pele waiting," I added.

"Oh crap, not that again," Collin moaned.

Collin's countenance shut down. His normal, placid, non-emotional mask clouded with aggravation.

"Where did you get that?" he asked.

Nobody said anything for an awkward moment before all eyes turned to Clark.

"What? Somebody from the department emailed it. It's fun."

Collin grunted, and with a turn, he was out the door—and out of the trailer— the door banging shut behind him.

"Well, that's kind of cool," I said to the space he had abandoned.

Leia looked at me. Her eyes tightened, the surrounding muscles contracted until she was almost squinting. "I didn't think I'd ever agree with you, but you're right. It is kind of cool."

"Someone should go tell him," I said.

"What? That we think him being the star of a comic strip when he was three is interesting?" Clark asked.

Leia started, "That he has shown an affinity to the earth, to the earth's needs since he was a child, and that being in a comic is actually kind of like being a celebrity."

Bro crossed his arms and chuckled. "This happens every semester, and no one has been able to convince him otherwise."

"Has anyone ever even tried?" I asked.

Everyone shrugged at the same time.

Maybe this was my in. Maybe if I could convince Collin that stardom— no matter how fleeting or how minor— was something pretty nifty.

It's not like I didn't know how to deal with fame. Well, at least I had at one point in time. Maybe not in this body, or this century.

"No one's going to go talk to him right now about it. Everybody, get back to work." Leia spoke with reason and authority.

Sadie and Clark let out annoyed sighs as they had to put down the exciting distraction of the moment and get back to data crunching.

I may have joined them with an overly loud exhalation of breath. With a shrug, I turned to head outside.

"You're not following him, are you?" Leia asked.

I pointed at the door. "Only in that I have to go outside. I am not going out there to talk to—"

"Dr. Paulo," she corrected before I could even say the man's name.

"Dr. Paulo about his brush with celebrity. I need to get a couple of those half-melted coolers that are stacked up next to the camper."

Her eyes went wide, and she nodded as I left.

I tried to ignore Collin, who was banging away on his computer under the tent, as I looked at the growing collection of half-melted coolers. I just needed something to help keep the GeoTalker cool while we were out close to the lava flows. Unlike Collin, Bro, and their students, my equipment was never designed to get that close to the heat.

I began stacking and twisting smaller coolers into larger ones before I found the perfect combination.

"Those aren't going to do you any good," Collin said. "They're too far damaged to form any kind of proper heat shielding."

I hefted the two coolers that I was carrying. They weren't horribly damaged. I figured if I twisted them—damage side to good side, front to back—I would be able to get decent enough heat shielding from them.

"They're better than nothing," I said. "And it's not like I can fabricate a proper heat shield."

When Bro recommended I try these out, I couldn't believe I had looked right past them as an option.

"If it doesn't work, then at least I can scientifically say I have eliminated this particular option."

Collin grunted. Back to typical Collin conversation. "You aren't going to try to talk me into thinking Pele and Pete is cool, are you?"

"I wasn't planning on it. Not today. It is, however, very cool."

"Yeah, but my name's not even Pete," he groused.

"No, but there's no rhyme or alliteration from Pele to Collin."

I wanted to ask him why it bothered him so much. Why didn't he embrace it? I mean, how incredibly cool would it be for a professor in volcanology, having been the star of a little comic about a little boy who tried to protect lava?

I shrugged and headed back inside.

As Leia said, now was not the time, and honestly, I didn't think Collin was going to be receptive anyway. He seemed to resent my presence, even when I didn't initiate conversation or try to ask him questions.

I spent the next couple of days brainstorming and building a better heat shield for the GeoTalker from a variety of the old ice chests. It took some trial and error, but in the end, I managed to concoct a heat shield that didn't also block the signal pulses that I was now quite interested in actually tracking.

"We're all headed up Kīlauea. It's supposed to be particularly active today. You want to grab a heat suit and join us?" Bro asked.

I glowered at the heat suit. It was like being a foil-wrapped baked potato and throwing myself directly on the coals. However, it was also a top-notch sauna and sweat bath.

"Do I want to? Not really. Do I need to? Yes, please," I said as I gathered my things. "I really need to get some better, more defined readings this week."

"What do you mean?"

"There seems to be a lot of— oh, I don't know." I shrugged. "I'm not sure what to call it. Background chatter?

Extra noises and signals I can't seem to identify. This would be a great chance for me to narrow in on what's going on."

I tucked the silver foil suit into my backpack and added the GeoTalker, safely nested in its double-walled heat shield, into the little wagon I had ordered to help me carry things around. I followed along as we all headed up toward the heart of the activity of Kīlauea.

Bro hung back with me. I gave his outfit a once over. Cargo shorts and flip-flops. "You aren't suiting up today?"

He shook his head. "I have to stay on terra firma for a while. My knee is acting up."

I glanced down at his shapely knee. I tilted my head as if it would help me focus. He frequently had an Ace bandage wrapped around his knee, but today he had what looked like bands of a bandage adhered directly to his skin. "What's on your knee?"

"Kinesthetic tape," he said proudly. "My physiotherapist gets all the latest and greatest techniques from Japan."

"Tape?" I asked.

"It works better than a bandage. Those provide compression. The tape can apply pressure, or help support the muscles in different ways. He explained it, all I care is that it works."

"Medical science for the win?" I asked, using a phrase I picked up from Sadie.

"Science for the win," he confirmed.

11

———

"Where should I set up?" I asked as soon as we arrived.

I had far less equipment than the grad students.

"We're going to be over this way," Bro said.

He pointed to an area that the day before had been neither solid nor liquid. Today, it was clear that a crust had formed over active lava. It was definitely not the kind of area I— or my untrained ass— needed to be in. I could be near the lava, but underneath my feet, it needed to be solid, dry ground. Not liquid ground.

As I lifted my cooler-wrapped GeoTalker from the back of the wagon, I looked for an area far enough away from the rest of the researchers so that their footfalls didn't send distracting signals to my equipment, but I also wanted to be close enough to the fresh lava flow that, if it was sending out any unique and specific signals, I would pick it up.

"Does that area right over there...?" I indicated a space just a few yards away from where I was unpacking. "Look okay?"

I asked anyone willing to answer, since technically they were all experts.

"You should be fine there. Uh..." Sadie said. She took a step closer to me, indicating with her hand what the living geology was doing around us.

"You can see how the flow was traveling in that direction," she said, "but it looks like it stopped. And now we have some active fire fountains further to the east— and everything seems to be flowing in that direction. I'd say over here is safe enough since most of the activity is over there. Keep an eye on it, though. These formations happened in the last week, they could do something unexpected on us."

I looked her square in the eye. "Can't you tell it's going to do anything unexpected?" I asked.

This conversation needed to be happening with Bro, or Collin.

"I'm not Dr. Paulo," she said flatly.

"None of us are," Bro said with a smirk.

I looked him square in the eye, then slightly behind him where Collin was working, before I darted my eyes back to meet his and gave him a weak smile.

"Hopefully, that's the kind of information this little GeoTalker and my research will be able to figure out for you guys— that maybe it isn't unpredictable. Maybe we just don't understand. We just can't read the signals it's sending to tell us what it's going to do next."

"What do you think?" I asked Collin once I noticed that his attention was on our conversation.

Collin shrugged.

"She's right," Bro said. "These flows— they're all a couple of days old, and they should be stabilizing. You can tell by the crystal formations. That sparkling... Hot lava has a different sheen to it when there's an active flow just a couple inches below the surface. You should be good there."

I smiled and nodded at both of them. I had equipment to set up and a foil suit to get kitted out in. It was time to turn myself into a foil-wrapped mad scientist.

My legs began sweating the second I stepped into the suit. It was a good thing we were required to wear long pants and long sleeves whenever we worked this close to the lava flows, or the Mylar-like aluminum fabric would have stuck to my sweaty shins like cling wrap.

As I continued to suit up, I watched one of the grad students— already wrapped for baking— tentatively step closer to the free-flowing lava. They extended some kind of wand that I knew was taking temperature readings. They were the true mad scientists. Getting out there. Living on the edge. Danger within reason, all for the sake of information.

Another foil-wrapped individual stepped in close, grabbed them by the arm, and pulled them several feet away — just as the rock where the student had been standing rolled and dissolved into the hot, flaming red molten earth.

That must have been Collin coming to the rescue. After all, he was supposed to have some second sense about all of this. I was sure that's why his parents' friend chose him to be the star of that little comic when he was barely more than a toddler.

"Is everyone okay?" I yelled out, not knowing if anyone in the other group would hear me over the unexpected roar that moving molten lava made.

I got a couple of thumbs up, so at least somebody heard me. I lifted my own thumb into the air, acknowledging their signal, before I put my helmet on.

I finished setting the GeoTracker up to run and turned on the small recording device with it before closing the lid to the cooler. I then put on my helmet. It was time to get toasty.

The air was hot and stifling once I was completely enclosed. Not that it wasn't hot out on the lava flow, but there was a surprising breeze keeping it from feeling stagnant. It was more like being in a convection oven than roasting over a fire. A lot of heat. Far too much heat for what I should have called my delicate constitution. But my constitution was taking a back seat to my yearning to regain my scientific brain.

I didn't need to be right on top of it. I checked my remote reader to see if a signal was coming through before I picked up the whole unit to deliver it a couple of yards closer to where Pele, the volcano goddess, was showing off in all of her glory.

I set the cooler down, keeping my eyes on the reader in my hands as I took several steps backward.

On my last step, the ground felt squishy. I pivoted.

Everything happened all at once.

Bro roared my name, and then he was shouting for Collin.

I pivoted so I could look down at what I was stepping on, and then out of nowhere I was tackled around the middle and dragged several yards away.

I landed on my ass and back with a loud oof, the air knocked out of my lungs. The monitoring reader device flew from my hands. I could barely move with the large body resting on top of me. I couldn't even appreciate how our bodies were pressed together at the hips, my mind too concerned with my equipment.

He rolled off me and I turned to scramble toward the monitoring device, but before I could get to it, the other person grabbed me again and pulled me back even farther.

His "No!" was loud, even through the natural barrier and muffling of his helmet.

I watched in horror as the ground where I had been standing dissolved from seemingly solid black rock to bubbling, boiling, red death.

"The GeoTalker!" I yelled, squirming out of his grip.

The ground beneath me felt wobbly as I got to my feet. I couldn't tell if that was an earthquake, volcanic activity, or just the aftereffects of being tackled by a large man. I may not have been able to see his face, but I could tell by the shape of the person inside the foil suit that it wasn't Clark—who was tall and skinny— this was Collin. If Bro was also suited up, I wouldn't have been able to distinguish between the two men.

"Get back! Get back! Damn it, Mancey, back off," Collin yelled.

Finally listening, I turned and ran in the direction he indicated. I really wanted to run and grab my GeoTalker, but I knew I was neither nimble nor strong enough to grab it and make it out before lava consumed me. By the time I got to where I knew the ground was more stable, Collin was next to me, dumping what was left of a now mostly melted cooler that had once held my GeoTalker.

I dropped to my knees and began tearing at my cooling device to see if anything had survived. I couldn't do anything with those awkward gloves on. I tore them off and tentatively touched the sides of the cooler to see if it was going to burn me or not. It was hot, but I hardly noticed in my frantic need to check my equipment.

I broke at least one fingernail ripping into the thing and didn't feel like I could breathe until I saw that the GeoTalker was happily ticking away inside.

Only then did I turn and pull my helmet off.

"You saved me," I said, looking into the fathomless depths of Collin's eyes. "You saved me."

"Is the equipment okay?" Collin asked. His chest heaved.

"I don't know." I carefully checked everything as I continued to review all of it. "It's still collecting data."

I sat back on my haunches and started laughing. It was still collecting, still working.

"That's good, because your equipment looks ancient. I don't know if we'd be able to replace it or not."

"The equipment is new. I built it myself. But yeah, I don't know if I could get— or where I would get— the components again. Thank you," I said, feeling the words from deep down.

I cleared my throat. "Thank you," I said again, and I meant it.

As I looked at him— both of us sitting there in our heat-protection suits, looking like so much wadded-up tin foil, I felt that familiar pull and tinkling in my gut again. Maybe it was the light refracting off his foil suit, but I swear Collin was sparkling like he had the first time I had met him.

12

———

"Whoo! What a day. Are you sure you're okay? That was a close call. Were you able to gather much data?" Sophie asked as we all settled back into more comfortable clothes of shorts and T-shirts.

I shrugged. "I can't really tell from what I've got here," I admitted, "but I definitely was able to collect."

"Is it going to be useful?" she asked as we unpacked our equipment and settled back into the trailer after the excitement out at the lava flow.

Of course, once me and my equipment were safely back on solid ground, the rest of the field work went off without a hitch with no additional heart-pounding moments of near misses with the molten red stuff.

"I got some strong recordings," I said, "but I don't know if it's even going to be viable data or not."

I began checking over the GeoTalker. Nothing looked broken, but I noticed a few connections had gotten loose. I pulled out the small tool kit I kept and began working. The reliability of my data was only as good as my equipment.

"And if it's not?" she asked.

I shrugged. "Then I'm back out with you the next time you take a field trip to the lava flow."

As I reviewed the data I'd gathered, I had some strong readings. At first, I had some clear signals from Kīlauea letting us know she was on the move. But then, the readings became less clear, and I couldn't tell if the garbled data I had collected was because the GeoTalker had been thrown around— or if I was getting chatter from something else, somewhere else.

Where we were located on the island was situated about halfway between Mauna Loa and Mauna Kea. Mauna Loa had been active enough several years ago, it wasn't out of line to think she was making noise too.

"Did I break your box?" Collin asked as he banged into the trailer.

I stopped tightening the connections between the old transistors and vacuum tubes, and blinked up at him. It was great to finally have him talking to me about our mutual work.

"No. It looks like everything is holding up just fine," I admitted. "But I don't know if the readings I've been getting are garbled because other parts of the island are getting noisy, or if there is some damage I haven't been able to identify."

"Then we need to eliminate some of your variables," he offered.

My insides gave a little flutter when he said *we*.

"Yeah, we do," I admitted. "But first I have to identify those variables and then be able to take direct readings from them."

"That should be easy enough," he said. "We have four active volcanoes on the island, right? Why not go directly to the others and see what kind of readings you get? Would you be able to identify the patterns of a different volcano in order to eliminate them from the background noise of what you just collected?"

I blinked a few times at the obviousness of his solution.

Why hadn't I thought of that?

"If I could get in close, I should be able to identify them. That would be two theory-birds with one stone." I held up my pointer finger. "Do different volcanoes have different signal patterns?" I asked, holding up a second finger. "And if they do, can I identify them to clear them out of the background noise from all of this?" I gestured wildly at the GeoTalker.

"Problem is, I don't have an easy way to get to those locations," I admitted. I quirked my lips to the side and lifted my brows.

"What do you mean, you don't have an easy way to get to those locations?"

Clearly, Collin hadn't been paying much attention to my situation.

"I ride a bike to and from the campground every day. I don't think I could pedal my way across the island in a timely fashion." It may have only been about seventy-five miles wide, and I'm sure there were plenty of cyclists who could do that without blinking an eye, but that was not me. I had issues with hills. Hell, I had issues with flats. While I could remember how to ride a bike, it seemed that Addison had never. And I was stuck with her physical muscle memory, not my own.

"I could give you a ride," he offered. "We just need a free afternoon. I can run you up to Mauna Kea. How much time do you need to get a good reading?"

I shrugged and grimaced. "An hour or two? Longer is better, but if there is a signal, that should be enough time."

"An hour or two," he repeated. "Let's set it, then. Tomorrow, you and me. We'll head out to Mauna Loa and if time, Mauna Kea or Hualālai, and see if you can pick up any other active readings."

My stomach twisted in an absolute knot. I was going to spend an entire day with Collin. A stupid grin spread across my face. Data collecting on old volcanoes may not seem romantic to some people, but to me, it was a prime opportunity.

It turned out to be a prime opportunity for precisely nothing— unless we were talking specifically about the volcanoes and lava flows. Collin's conversation went nowhere. And that glimmer of sparkle on his skin? Sweat or left over glitter from a performance. Nothing about him sparkled.

I wanted to make a smart, supportive comment about his feelings regarding Pele and Pete, but there was never a natural opening. I didn't think it was a good volley to just immediately start talking about something he declared he didn't like. The only thing I think he said voluntarily to me was to ask if I was wearing sunscreen.

When we got to the top of Mauna Loa, I expected him to pitch in, offer help, offer suggestions, as he had the day before. But he just leaned against his truck and watched as I did all the heavy lifting and data gathering.

The ride from Mauna Loa to Mauna Kea was as tedious as tedious got. When I attempted to get him to talk about dance, it was as if he thought his competition dancing was as embarrassing or unimportant as him being featured in a comic when he was a small child.

"How long have you been dancing?" I asked.

He shrugged. "All my life."

"Well, that would explain... That would explain why you're so strong."

He grunted. Couldn't the man take a compliment? He was infinitely interesting— he was an award-winning competition dancer, he starred in a comic as a kid. His sister was Emmy nominated. Yet, he brushed everything off as if it were normal. Didn't he realize his normal was not the experience of everyone else?

"How long have you known Dr. Nakamura?" I tried a different approach. "Did you meet because of the geology or the dancing?"

"I don't know. Both." He shrugged again and turned his face away from me.

I don't think I made it to twenty minutes of this question-and-one-word-answer session before I gave up. At least gathering data at Mauna Loa offered something more interesting. Though the volcano wasn't currently in high activity, it was still active enough and kicking up readings. I was fairly certain there was an identifiable pattern here that I would be able to filter out from the readings from Kīlauea.

Mauna Loa had been chatty. Mauna Kea had been silent.

Turns out Collin was also silent. And not the strong stoic silent type, but the watching-mold-grow-is-more-interesting-than-you silent type.

Any interest Collin had in me and my research ended after he drove me around the island to gather more recordings. He didn't seem to care whether I had discovered that there was— or was not— an identifiable signal from either volcano that I could then filter out of my readings.

He wasn't interested, even though there was a direct correlation to supporting his theories and research.

But Bro was.

And he was there, flashing his very shapely knees at me when we returned.

"Any luck?" he asked, interrupting my calculations, of course.

I was nose-down in a notebook, running calculations by hand.

"Actually," I said, smiling up at him. "A lot of luck. It appears that Kīlauea is sending out a unique signal, as is Mauna Loa."

"And Mauna Kea?" he asked.

"Mauna Kea is completely silent."

"It is dormant, so no surprise there. Did you make it out to Hualālai?"

"I shook my head. "No."

"Too bad, it's been quiet for a while, but it would be nice to know what it's thinking about. What did you find?"

I pointed to lists of digits, which to me were obviously signal patterns, but to anybody else— and possibly to Bro— were just lists of numbers. But as a research scientist, I expected him to understand that deep in those numbers was something I could see.

"There's... there's something else in here. I've been able to eliminate the strongest of the background noises, but there's still a lot of— I don't know— geological chatter going on."

"Well, we are a volcanic archipelago. You could probably collect readings from other volcanoes and eliminate them."

"Well, where would be the next closest volcano I could get a reading from that's not on the island?"

He exposed his teeth with a hiss. "Ah, crap, it's Loihi." His lips twisted up in a half-smirk, then he cocked one eyebrow at me and tilted his head. "How are you for deep sea diving?"

"Oh," I groaned. "You've got to be kidding me."

He shook his head. "I'm not. The closest volcano is underwater."

"Yeah, that's not gonna happen," I said. "I am not, nor do I care to be, scuba certified. And sorry, you're not getting me into a submersible. Where's the next closest volcano I can set foot on?"

He shrugged. "After Hualālai? Maui. We could check out Hualālai and if that's not helpful we could go to Haleakalā, and see if that's where your noise is coming from. See if that's generating some of the noise you've got."

"I think Collin is done driving me around. I guess I could get a car for the day, but Maui?" I asked. "Okay... there isn't a ferry or some kind of boat shuttle, is there?"

He shook his head. "No. If we want to go to Maui, we're flying."

"Great. Great. Another day of travel just to gather a couple hours' worth of data." I must have groaned or something.

"You're not looking forward to the flight?"

I shook my head. "Not looking forward to having to lug that on and off of airplanes."

"Well, I could go with you and do the heavy lifting," he suggested.

I narrowed my eyes at him.

"Dr. Paulo offered to drive me around this island so that I could collect data from the other volcanoes."

"And that's exactly what he did," Bro continued my thought for me. "And that's all he did, isn't it?"

I nodded my head slowly, admitting that that *is* all Collin did. There was little to no conversation, no camaraderie, and I didn't know if I would call his presence company or not. Whatever I had seen in him, it was clearly limited to two things— his good bone structure and his physicality when it came to dancing. He had the personality of a piece of cold volcanic rock.

There had been something interesting there once. Now, it was just a piece of cooled lava. Interesting to the right rock collector. And while there was something vaguely interesting about that, it wasn't nearly as interesting as the hot stuff.

On the other hand, Bro ran hot. Really hot.

13
———

As soon as we disembarked, Bro announced he couldn't lift anything heavier than five pounds. "Doctor's orders. Or my shoulder won't recover." He was covered in that physiology tape again. Strips of tape that were a high contrast pale color against his rich brown tones poked out from under the sleeve of his shirt, and were wrapped over only one of his knees.

Fortunately, the GeoTalker and its case didn't weigh too much, and the cooler had a functional handle.

We didn't waste any time and grabbed a ride straight to the base of the volcano's pumice cone. After all, this was a research work trip. I was here to gather data, not to go sightseeing, and certainly not to have an extended lunch with Emi— which, if I had been on my own, is exactly what I would have been doing.

I wanted to know all the gritty details of her newly married life and skyrocketing career as George O'Connell's smart-witted, badass, local sidekick on TV.

After setting the GeoTalker up, Bro sat idly watching me.

"How long before you think you'll get enough data?" he asked as I set the device in place.

I glanced down at the GeoTalker and pulled out my phone. I still may not have been able to successfully run calculations on my fancy new tablet, but I was a whiz at the smartphone thing, especially the scheduler.

"I should have all the data I need in the next two hours and thirty-five minutes," I announced.

"That's very precise," Bro said.

"Oh," I shrugged, "because we have to leave for the airport for our flight home in exactly two hours and forty-five minutes, and it's going to take about ten minutes to get this thing packed back up once it's done its job of talking to the volcano."

The laugh he let out rumbled deep through his chest.

Doing this little field trip with Bro was a complete polar opposite experience from my little field trip with Collin. The extent of Collin's conversation had been nothing more than a series of grunts, and I certainly don't remember if he laughed at anything I had said.

Bro pushed up to his feet and began kicking around in the dirt. I was distracted by his actions and just watched him. His movements were paced and regular. It took me a second to realize he was dancing. He may not have been doing the full movements, but he was marking time in his head. He was so different. So appealing. So not Collin.

I gritted my teeth, growled a little bit deep in my throat, and refocused my energy on setting up and getting the GeoTalker ready to start collecting data. I could wax poetic about my attraction for Bro over Collin once this was done.

Then again— as I shot another glance up to Bro, he turned at the same time the muscles in his arms bunched and flexed as he positioned them over his head, and brought them down to slap his hands against his thighs. His lips twitched up in a half grin, and then he winked at me.

The nerves in my stomach cavorted about— not unlike they had earlier on the airplane— only those had scared me. If I was truthful with myself, these nerves scared me even more.

"What ever shall we do while your little toy collects data?"

I ignored him. As soon as I saw everything was working, I stood and faced him. "It's not a toy."

He stepped closer. "I know, but you're cute when you get riled up. I like the way your nose scrunches up." He playfully bopped me on my nose.

I opened my mouth to say something, but was silenced as his lips slid across mine. His kiss felt like the buzz of static electricity.

"Oh," I sighed into his mouth. "Are you sure this is such a good idea?"

"I can't think of a better way to spend the next two hours and twenty minutes. Can you?"

I stretched my arms over his shoulders and twisted my fingers into his hair. "You are a very smart man."

"I have the degrees to prove that. But it doesn't take a PhD to know that I need to shut up and kiss you more."

"Yes you do."

And he did exactly that. He may have had higher level academic degrees in geology, but he was a master artisan when it came to kissing. He knew exactly how much pressure and when. His lips slid over mine, and he knew exactly when to tease me with the tip of his tongue.

I parted my lips for him to deepen the kiss, and plunder my mouth. I nibbled at his lower lip before offering my tongue to him. He sucked on me and stole my breath.

He crushed me against his chest, and I clutched at his massive shoulders, and grabbed handfuls of hair. I wanted him closer. I wanted him touching my skin. My entire body felt like liquid fire.

I didn't care if Collin had an affinity for lava. It was Bro who turned me into molten flesh. He was the true master of heat and desire. Bro was the one who had the favor of the gods, he was the one who made me glow and radiate, and want to explode. And that was just with his lips against mine, and his touch through a few thin layers of fabric.

I needed to know what he could do skin on skin. Probably burn me alive.

A timer sounded somewhere, and he finally stepped away from me. His mouth was red and his lips slightly swollen from our aggressive make out session.

"We should continue this later," he said as his breath made his chest heave with panting effort.

We were both panting from the heated effects of our kisses.

"Yeah," I agreed. I tried to slick my hair behind my ear as I turned my attention back to the GeoTalker and check on the progress of the data collection— the reason for the interrupting alarm.

The space inside the plane was tight to begin with, and I swear the seats were even smaller than on the flight earlier that morning. My sizable hips felt as if they were wedged in. Even if I had been willing to spend the money and suggested an upgrade to first class, this plane didn't have one.

It was affectionately termed a puddle jumper. And the fact that— even now, in the twenty-first century— there was a plane with propeller engines... One would think that even though I was used to mid-century airplanes, the fact that we were flying in a tin can with propeller engines did not settle my nerves.

Of course, the press of Bro's shapely knees leaning against my leg was not helping me any.

The plane shimmied and jumped, and I let out a little gasp. I immediately looked out the window. There were minimal clouds, and the sky was clear.

"Why is there so much turbulence?" I asked.

"I didn't take you for a nervous flyer," Bro commented.

He rested his large, warm hand on my forearm, where I had a death grip on the armrest between us. I twisted my arm around so that I could grab onto him.

The plane shimmied again. "Apparently I am totally a nervous flyer, especially in these little planes."

I could picture the pilot with a wide, crazy grin, shouting, "Yee-haw!" as he purposefully swooped the plane around like some form of seabird. There was only a heavy blue curtain between the cockpit and the passenger section. And considering I didn't hear anybody making gratuitous and enthusiastic daredevil noises, I was sure I was superimposing visions from my memories of what were now considered old-time movies over my active imagination.

"As somebody who's been working in the field with a bunch of volcanologists, I would think you'd be a little better versed in thermal dynamics. You don't need clouds to have wind."

"I'm a communications specialist," I nervously giggled as I tried to remind him. "I pick up signals and see if they might be some form of translatable language. I don't study rocks and heat."

"Besides—" I sucked in a small gasp, this time feeling a change of pressure in my stomach-- "I would think that someone so focused on what's going on under the earth's core would be just as much at a loss as I am about what's going on in the atmosphere."

I suppressed a nervous moan as the sinking feeling grew stronger.

"Why couldn't we have done this by boat? Why aren't there ferries from island to island?"

I looked out the window again.

"Is the ocean getting closer?" I asked, trying to suppress my nerves.

"There aren't any ferries because—" he began. And as he spoke, I learned far more about Hawaii's determination to preserve its ecological uniqueness and diversity from island to island than I had ever paid any attention to. Ferries transported nonpaying guests, and the last thing anybody wanted was the wrong kind of snake or rat to make its way to a new location and cause havoc, or worse wipe out a local endangered population of anything. There were environmental concerns of oils and gasses impacting the local sea life, from coral reefs to the local whale population. Long story short, the boats and their pollutants were not healthy for the region.

"You really are having a hard time right now, aren't you?"

I nodded my head. "I didn't realize I was claustrophobic," I said, as my gaze darted around the very small cabin. The extent of these nerves was new to me.

"What do you mean, you didn't think you were claustrophobic?"

I waved my hand in circles in front of my neck, attempting to cool off.

"I have some memory issues as a result of an accident. I don't know how much you heard at Emi's wedding," I started to explain. "And sometimes there are aspects of my life before that show up rather unexpectedly..."

"You have amnesia?" Bro asked.

I shrugged. "Kind of. In a way. There are some things I remember better than others," which was mostly a lie. But then again, not really. I, Mancey, remembered a whole hell of a lot of things about my glamorous life as a starlet, but I, Mancey, very much did not remember things from the life of this body. Addison's history was a mystery to me. And she was crap at filling me in on pertinent information.

If there wasn't a photograph in one of those albums that Kristen had insisted on showing me, I had next to no way of knowing anything about Addison or her history in this body. Addy tended to run away when I needed her input, like now.

Maybe what I was feeling was residual muscle memory coming back. I didn't have a problem on the earlier flight. I couldn't remember having a problem on the flight after the accident, returning to Idaho. And I certainly didn't have any issues on the flight back to Hawaii. Then again, that plane had been substantially larger, and I had booked a first-class passage.

"Oh," I let out a nervous whimper.

"That fast, dropping sensation you're feeling," Bro practically chuckled. "We are getting closer to the ocean. We're descending."

I really did not like this onset of panicked emotion. I was a smart woman. I was in control of my life. This felt very out of my hands.

"The ocean is getting closer, but that's only because we're coming in for a landing."

"We're already back?" I asked incredulously. I hadn't had a moment to enjoy being pressed next to Bro this time. "But I thought we had just gotten to cruising altitude."

"Well, there's a reason they call planes like this puddle

jumpers. They basically go up and then come right back down."

"Don't say it like that." I gulped down the panic that insisted on making its presence known.

"Sorry. Let me rephrase. They basically go up and then come down in a controlled descent. It's not a long flight."

"It's long enough," I complained.

"Not nearly long enough," Bro said. His lids lowered as his gaze darkened. His eyes flashed to my lips and back up.

I gulped. "Long enough for what?"

He tilted his head to the side and shrugged before running his hand over my arm and shifting his leg so that our thighs slid against each other. "I could think of a way to distract you, but we didn't get high enough."

"High enough?" I asked.

"Mile high," he smirked.

It took me entirely too long to get his reference. The mile-high club. Not in a plane that had no privacy, not in a plane this small. I blushed.

"High enough? What about long enough? We're barely in the air long enough for a quickie," I whispered, lowering my voice even more so than I had been. People didn't need to hear our conversation, and we didn't need to impinge on their listening space.

Bro laughed. "I see you have kept your wicked sense of humor, even if you are all nerves."

"Who said I was being funny?" I tried to apply my femme fatale skills to the conversation, even though I still had a death grip on the arm rest.

"Now you're being a tease," he said. His smoldering expression stayed hot on my face.

"You started this to distract me. I'm simply pointing out the flaw in your little plan. This is not the plane for that sort of activity. However, I am interested in seeing what you had in mind."

"See, tease," he said. "This conversation is completely inappropriate between professor and student."

"I seem to recall you made it a point to let me know you are not my academic advisor," I reminded him.

"You're right, I'm not. And you are still a tease."

I shook my head. "Not a tease, an invitation. Brody Nakamura, would you like to accompany me back to my cabin after we land?"

14

———————

I set the cooler with the GeoTalker inside down and fumbled in my messenger bag for the door key. It rattled around in the lock, a poor fit from years of abuse.

The door opened and Bro let out a low whistle. "You have to step outside to change your mind."

I reached in and grabbed the handle bars and dragged my bike onto the porch.

"It's a lot bigger when the bike isn't inside," I admitted.

This wasn't going nearly as smoothly or as seductively as I had hoped. There had been plenty of furtive glances on the ride over from the airport, but I wasn't quietly leading him by the hand into my bedroom, where he could do with me what he had hinted at.

No, I had to wrestle with the cheap lock before hauling my bike outside.

"I have a chain lock, but I figured if I was going to be gone for the day, it would be safer inside," I said as I continued to pull the bike the rest of the way out and retrieved the chain and lock from the basket.

Bro watched as I locked the bike to the pole that held up the roof.

Once finished with that, I kick-pushed the cooler across the threshold and into my small living space. With a flourish of my hands, I indicated that Bro should step inside.

"Before I step inside, we should agree that we should keep this between us. While technically not against any fraternization rules..."

I nodded in understanding. "We aren't breaking any rules, but we should still not flaunt whatever this is in front of the others. Understood. After you," I followed him in and clicked the lights on before closing the door.

Bro turned and stepped into me. I fell back against the door.

He boxed me in with his hands braced against the door on either side of me. The noise he made low in his throat was more like a purr than a growl. Whatever it was, it sent a shiver up and down my spine and made my toes curl in my shoes. His face was so close to mine, the tip of his nose brushed lightly across my cheek and along my jaw.

My heart pounded into my throat. The anticipation of having Bro's hands on me had my pulse racing, and my breath stuttering in my chest.

He reached out and flicked the light off. "I don't think we are going to need this. There is enough light in here for me to see what I'm doing."

Considering I had my eyes closed, I didn't care if the lights were on or not. All I needed was to feel Bro's closeness. I didn't need illumination to run my hands over his pecs and shoulders. He was a wall of solid muscle.

"I want to feel your skin," I managed to whimper.

He trailed his finger along my jaw and tipped my chin up. "Look at me, Mancey," he directed.

I was his to command. My lids fluttered open.

"Are you sure about this? Because I want to do much more than simply kiss you."

There was nothing simple about the way he had kissed me earlier. His kisses were complex and layered. There were nuances in his technique that would take me years to properly study.

"I am the one who invited you back to my cabin," I reminded him. Twisted my fingers in the hem of his t-shirt. "Can I please touch you?" I pleaded.

He didn't step away from me to remove his shirt. His arms brushed against my curves and skimmed over my breasts as he reached the shirt over his head. He tossed it away and pressed in tighter to me. "Is this better?"

I let out a sigh as my palms came into contact with his warmth. "It would be even better if you were kissing me."

"Say no more." And then his lips slid over mine.

Bro pressed the length of his body against mine. He ran a hand down my side and over my hip. Fingers bit into my thigh as he hiked my leg up to his hip. I was caught between him and the door at my back, which was good because my knees were going weak from his kisses, and I was quickly losing the ability to hold myself up.

I moaned into his mouth as he devoured my kisses. And to think I had thought his kisses earlier on the side of the volcano had been potent. That had been nothing compared to how he was laying waste to my very essence.

He began slowly pulling us away from the support of the door. We turned slowly through space as if we were dancing until my legs bumped against the bed. Slowly, artfully, with a display of strength, Bro lowered us to the bed. There was no sudden drop with the force of gravity. It felt like the magic of the seduction finally arrived after the awkwardness of wrestling to get inside the cabin.

Bro's hands, no longer needing to hold me up, began running over me. He skimmed electrical shocks as his fingers grazed across my skin. And his touch was more forceful when there were clothes between his touch and my body.

As he distracted me with more kissing, I explored the ridges and terrain of the muscles of his arms and shoulders. His body was like a sculpture, artistic, beautiful, rock hard.

He ran his hands under the hem of my skirt and began pushing it out of the way.

"Buttons," I panted out. "Buttons."

He hummed and pulled away from the kiss. He knelt over me and began unfastening the buttons of my shirt. In the low light, his eyes gleamed. The light and shadows made his features seem sharper, more pronounced. He was stunning.

I wriggled beneath his fingers. He spread my shirt open and let out a rush of breath as he gazed over my breasts.

"Are those for me?" he asked with deep gravel in his voice.

"All of me is for you," I said breathlessly. The way he looked at me was driving me almost as crazy as his touch was.

I wanted to be fully on display for him. I pushed up onto my elbows and twisted to unfasten my bra.

Bro watched as I flung my bra to the side. He started to reach for me, but then I fumbled with the closure on my cargo shorts. I had embraced the grad student uniform, it was practical and functional, and I had long given up trying to be the center of attention.

Bro hooked his fingers in the waist band at my hips and

slowly began dragging my pants down. He let out another hiss of appreciation as I was fully exposed.

"You are a bounty, and I don't know where to start," he said in a low whisper.

"I'm not going anywhere, but maybe you start by losing your shorts. I feel like I'm missing out by not getting to see all of you."

Bro jumped from the bed and pushed out of his pants. His erection sprung forth, glorious and ready for service.

I may have hissed in a similar fashion. He was so beautiful and willing to share all of that with me. I held my arms out to him, beckoning him back to me. The gracefulness of his movements were not abandoned as he returned to my embrace. He moved with an unworldly smoothness that spoke volumes of his physical training as a dancer. He knew how to move and use his body, both for his art and in bed. His kisses left me breathless, even when he wasn't directly stealing the air from my mouth. The simple act of his lips against my skin was enough for me to forget how to think.

My limbs alternated between being limp and boneless, to being entirely too heavy to move, to being light and liquid as my touch flowed around him.

He was right, where to start when there was so much fun to be had in touching and tasting. I wanted him over me, I wanted him under me. I wanted my lips wrapped around his length, and I wanted his lips against mine. There were simply too many options. And while we had all night to play and explore, I wanted it all at once.

We touched and rubbed our bodies together. The slide of him was like silk over my skin. He touched and explored my skin with his fingers and mouth. I was left gasping and mewing when he finally found a nipple with his tongue. He flicked and twirled the tip of it around, driving me crazy, and encouraging my nipple to peak and harden.

All the touching and caressing had been building up. It may have only been his mouth on my breast, but it was the switch that activated my core. I was already tightening up in anticipation of him sliding into me, but this was like lightning through my body.

"Oh gods, I need you," I whimpered.

"I'm right here," his voice was as sexy as his touch. I was going to orgasm simply from the sound of his words.

"More, I need more of you. I need you in me." I was desperate. I was not going to survive any more soft touches and heated licks and soft nibbles. I was going to explode, and when I did, I needed to feel him deep inside.

He reached a hand between us and stroked my sex. "You want me here?"

I rocked my hips against his hand. "Yes," I moaned.

His fingers slipped between my folds and slid back and forth, stroking me, teasing me. It felt so good, but I wanted his cock.

"You are so wet. I bet you're already tight and pulsing."

I whimpered.

"Let's make sure you're good and ready," he said before returning his mouth to my nipple. He sucked in time with the soft stroking of his fingers.

"I'm ready, I'm so ready." I just needed him to slide a finger in, and I would lose what little hold I had on keeping my body at bay.

Fortunately, I didn't have to wait or plead anymore. He slid the head of his thick cock against me. When it bumped my clit, the first surge of release coursed through my body. I was already clenching and losing my mind when he slid into me.

"Damn woman, you were already partying without me."

I didn't have it in me to respond with an 'I told you so.' I was too lost in the sensations of my body wrapping around him and pulling him in deeper. I had no breath to scream with, only whimper and mew as I crashed over and over again.

His touch felt like energy surging through my body. He rocked into me, pressing our hips together over and over. He needed to catch up because I was limp and worthless as my body was wrung out in its attempts to pull everything from him.

I gasped and panted and held on as he drove me well over the edge again and again. He growled his own release before slowing his motions. He didn't stop, not for a few more thrusts. I didn't know if I could have survived more, even if he had been able to continue.

I shook with muscle fatigue and exhaustion. There was no way this body had ever experienced anything so outstanding. I couldn't remember a time that I had in my previous life. "Oh shit, that was, amazing."

Bro lay on his back, his chest lifting and falling with his own exertion. "I don't have words. Come here."

He pulled me against him, so that I collapsed across his chest.

"Better," he murmured before I slipped into a dreamless sleep.

15

———

My heart was in my throat. I couldn't believe what I was looking at.

I ran the calculation again. No, it was there. A distinct and unique pattern of electrical pulses that I could trace back to specific volcanoes. Moana Loa was chattering differently from Kīlauea, and by deduction the other line of data had to be Loihi.

Both Moana Kea and Haleakalā were silent. Completely silent.

"Are you all right? You look a little flushed and excited." Bro added a cheeky eyebrow lift and a wink. "What did I do this time?"

I swat the air in his direction. "Stop it." I giggled.

"Ugh," Leia complained in the background. "We have flies inside again?"

For a split second, I flushed with indignation. She was always going on about how unprofessional and too familiar I was with Collin, but did she just call Bro a fly? It took me a second to realize there were bugs darting around in the front part of the trailer near the kitchen area.

She wasn't commenting on my flirting.

Bro snorted out a laugh. "Ignore her," he said to me. His face got more serious, but his lips are still twitched up in a soft grin. "Our little trip to Maui helped?"

I showed him a line of numbers.

He shrugged. "They're all the same. No variation."

"Exactly," I practically gushed. It was just too perfect. "It's a flat line. A flat line."

"That doesn't sound useful to me," Leia interjected. "Why are you so excited about a flat line?"

"Null data is just as useful as active data," Bro responded. "Failed hypotheses are just as valid, sometimes more so. I wish the scientific community would publish more articles of negative results. Proving something wrong is just as important." Bro's voice went flat, and he sounded like a college lecturer.

Which made sense, after all, this graduate field research was still technically a learning environment. And Bro was a professor, and a scientist.

"Mancey, please explain to Leia why gathering no data from Haleakalā is exciting."

"It means that active volcanoes potentially have identifiable energy signals. Dormant activity means dormant. So if suddenly there's a new signature signal, somebody is waking up. At least that's the theory that's evolving from all of this," I said.

"I thought you wanted to track earthquakes, tectonic plate movement?" Leia asked. She had turned away from her laptop and instead of reacting to my flirting with Bro, she was fully engaged with us now.

"That's the long game," I said with a nod. "I need something a little more active to demonstrate that there are signals being generated. Kīlauea is very chatty. Moana Loa is making noise, but its pattern is spaced further apart. But it is a pattern. And this other line I have is a pattern, and I think it has to be Loihi or Hualālai. Because null data proves it's not Muana Kea or Haleakalā." I cut my gaze away from Leia and up at Bro. "I need an isolated, active volcano. No extra chatter around."

His brow furrowed in thought. "Got a passport?"

I did. It was still under Addison Jones's name, but so were most of my documents. I hadn't actually gotten around to legally changing my name. I was just telling everyone I had, and living my best life without the shadow of Addison hanging over me.

I nodded slowly. "I'm going to have to take this on the road. Check out some other volcanoes."

"Well, you're in the right place for volcanoes," she said just before she stepped outside, and the door banged closed behind her.

I think that had been the most reasonable conversation I ever had with Leia. I shifted my gaze from down the hall to the front of the trailer to where Bro stood near me.

"I think you need different volcanoes," Bro said.

"Any ideas?" I asked. I wasn't up-to-date on where the active volcanoes were hanging out. I had never expected my GeoTalker to actually work, or for me to get invested in the research.

"I know exactly where we need to go, Tonga," Bro announced.

"Tonga? You're not serious, are you?"

Bro smirked at me as he leaned against my desk. "They have good beaches."

"We're in Hawaii. There are good beaches here. Also, in case you haven't noticed, I'm not exactly the beachy type."

"You just haven't been to the beach with someone who knows how to beach properly."

"Is that an invitation?" I lifted my brows. Was Bro asking me out?

"If you think hanging out on the side of a caldera tracking signals from an underwater volcano is an invitation, yes. I guess." He shrugged.

"Wait, what part of I don't dive did you forget?"

Bro shrugged again. "I didn't forget. The land mass is young and potentially not permanent. Hunga Tonga-Hunga Ha'apai went boom a few years ago and emerged between two islands that were technically the edges of the caldera. Probably no beach? If there is one, it's not a tourist location. I've been wanting to check it out. The island is made of ash that solidified. And it's a bit of an anomaly that it's still around."

"Went boom? That's a technical term?" My brain went blank, Tonga? "Why not Alaska, or, I don't know, aren't there volcanoes in Columbia? You know, some place that might need a bigger airplane to get to?"

"You want an active volcano, this is your best bet. Besides, I can get the department to cover this trip. It's research for me as well. It's perfect."

Nerves in my stomach flipped. Tonga. That meant a lot of time in an airplane. This new-found fear of flying wasn't something I was used to. And this onslaught of nerves while I wasn't even near an airplane, only thinking about it, wasn't doing me any favors.

"We'll be on a commercial flight to Fiji. You know, a big airplane. Only from Fiji to Tonga will we be in one of those little puddle jumpers," Bro said soothingly.

I cut my gaze to him and narrowed my eyes. Had he read my mind?

He smiled at my glare. "You're muttering. I don't think you realize you do that."

My eyes went wide. "I'm doing what?"

"You're muttering about not liking small planes. If your expression wasn't informative enough, you tend to softly talk to yourself when you're stressed. You'll be fine. I'll be right there with you."

"Yeah, you were there on the last plane, and I was still a bit of a mess," I admitted. "And I don't talk to myself." Or did I?

"You do, and I'll do a better job at distracting you."

"What do you have in mind?"

He gave me a half grin and a wink. "I'll have to think of something good."

16

I couldn't believe I had agreed to this. I couldn't believe I was acting like a Nervous Nelly. Whatever muscle memory was going on with these travel nerves was beginning to piss me off. I wasn't Addison. She wasn't even around to feed me with her memories. She hadn't been around for a while. So why was my stomach in knots with her issues?

I was already sitting in the airport lounge at the gate when Bro sauntered up.

The man didn't walk. He strutted, completely unencumbered and undeniably sexy.

My reaction to his presence explained the nerves I was experiencing better than the fearful thought of flying did. We were not going to have to keep our distance from each other, or pretend there was nothing between us, when we sparked together like electricity bouncing around inside a plasma ball.

"No bags?"

He shrugged. "I checked everything." He lifted his phone. "I've got everything I need right here."

When boarding was called, and I had to hike my carry-ons and backpack onto my shoulders to lug onto the plane, I suspected he had figured out this traveling thing far better than I had.

As a starlet, I had people who took care of my bags and entertainment during travel. Of course, back then, all I had to carry with me was a book, I had no other options for entertainment. Having to take care of my own travel needs was new to me. I clearly wasn't very good at it.

"Comfy?" I asked Bro as I stored one bag over head, and had to wrestle the other under my seat.

"Yeah I'm good." He smiled up at me from the comfort of his seat while he scrolled on his phone.

The plane was small, but nothing as small as the propeller driven puddle jumper we had been on the week before. I wanted to chastise him for not following through on his promise to keep me distracted. In the end, he really didn't need to.

"How much time before our next flight?" I asked as I felt the tell-tale lift in my stomach that we were already coming in for a landing in Oahu.

"We have plenty of time to make our connecting flight."

How did he know? He probably had everything on his phone. I was still stuck somewhere between having to hold a physical confirmation and having everything digital on my phone. I rummaged through my travel documents until I found the print with the itinerary on it.

"I thought you said you got your name changed. These all say Addison Rouche Jones," Bro said as he leaned over my shoulder.

"I haven't had time to get my name changed. There have been some legal hiccups regarding residence and stuff like that."

"Where are you from?" he asked.

"I'm from Idaho. I want to remain from there, not have residence there."

"But you're a student at the University of Idaho. I thought you were doing all of this research so you could take it back to Yellowstone. Now that's a big caldera to study."

"What? Yellowstone isn't a volcano," I responded. He was talking crazy.

"How the hell did you come up with a theory about tectonic signals communicating movement and not know that Yellowstone is an active super volcanic complex?"

I stared at him hard for a long moment. I had to tap into my memories of the park. Addy wasn't here to help. Did she even know? Yellowstone, Old Faithful, buffalo. I knew nothing about the park. Shit.

"That explains the geysers," I said, hoping I was right.

Bro chuckled. "Exactly. Did you sleep through a few classes?"

"Ah, yeah, slept, skipped school. It's a miracle I've come as far as I have academically." I lied through my teeth. Fortunately, I'm a good actress.

"That's what you meant when you said you couldn't remember a few things after that accident?"

I couldn't believe he remembered. "That's exactly the kind of thing I've lost from my memories."

That was a little too close, he was going to figure out I wasn't who I said I was if I wasn't more careful. I should look up everything I could on Yellowstone. A super volcanic complex? Amazing.

Avoiding any deeply personal conversations on the flight from Hawaii to Fiji ended up being easier than I had thought. I somehow managed to fall asleep. And I slept hard. I never did get to find out what Bro had planned for distracting me.

"That's us," I said as the overhead speakers announced a list of connecting flights.

"We should—"

"Shh," I cut Bro off. I tilted my head to the side like a puppy, trying to hear better. I don't know why I did that, but it helped.

"Continue to the passenger information desk at guest services..." The message repeated in several different languages.

"This way." I hiked my bags over my shoulder and followed the trickle of other passengers who apparently were also traveling to the same destination. The walk seemed to take forever, mostly because everyone was moving rather slow, and my bags did not want to stay on my shoulder.

"What do you think is going on?" I asked.

Bro shrugged. "Change in gate?"

"Why not just announce it." I fished my flight itinerary print out from the outer pocket of my carry on bag.

"Most people just keep that on their phone," Bro pointed out.

"Call me old-fashioned. I like a paper backup." As much as I embraced computers and the internet, I was still reluctant to give into it completely. There was a reason all of my notes were still recorded on paper first before I transcribed them into my notebooks.

"Which way?" Bro asked. The group we were following seemed to divide into two distinct groups as we came to a junction in the terminal gates.

Having never been in that airport before, I had no idea how these travelers knew exactly what to do. At least I couldn't figure it out until I saw the directional signage. It was placed relatively low— not hanging from the ceiling or anything like that where people wouldn't block it— and a big arrow directed us to guest services to the right.

"Ah, that way," he said as he caught sight of the sign at the same time.

We followed along and got into the appropriate line. Other travelers around us grumbled regarding the inconvenience. Mostly how they were going to miss their connecting flights, or how this was ruining their vacation. I didn't think having to speak to customer service was ruining anything.

When it was our turn, I leaned in and handed my ticket to the agent. "We're supposed to be headed to Tonga."

She looked at my printouts and then shook her head before sliding them back to me. "Not tonight, you aren't. You've been rebooked onto a flight tomorrow afternoon. Your ticket will be good for that flight."

"Why, what's going on?"

"Weather at your destination."

"It's that bad?" Bro asked.

I let out a dejected sign. I really wanted the travel portion of this little adventure to be over with.

"For the safety of our passengers and crew, it's been determined that no flights will be going in or out of Vava'U, Tonga."

"So what do we do?" I asked.

"You can make yourself comfortable here, or you can find a hotel for the night," she said. "You only need a valid passport to enter Fiji, and you have twenty-four hours until your flight."

I glanced over at Bro. His eyes were narrowed, and he

looked like he wanted to grumble as much as the guy behind us had been.

"Hotel it is then," I announced. "I'm not going to try to sleep in a busy airport. And I swear, sleeping on the flight just left me more tired. You don't have one of those tourist information centers in the airport, do you?"

With a nod, she pointed and gave directions on how we could find the next information desk that would be able to help us out.

"If this was a vacation, I would be bitching about it getting ruined," Bro muttered.

"Why? We get to spend the night in Fiji? I can't say that's something I ever thought I'd be doing."

"Yeah, Fiji, but at some airport hotel. You aren't going to be on the beach," he pointed out.

"For a few extra bucks, I bet we could be on the beach."

"More like a couple of hundred extra."

He wasn't wrong. It was a dramatic price difference to get a beachside room in one of those bungalow resorts. That made it much easier to insist on booking only one room. I was afraid Bro was going to insist on the airport hotel and having his own room.

17

───────

When I walked through the room and out the wide-open doors to my own private beach access, it was totally worth every penny spent. And I need to rethink my motivations. This place was so beautiful.

I had been living on a tropical island for almost six months, and I don't think I quite appreciated it as much as I did being in this hotel on a different island. When we got back to Hawaii, I was going to let Bro show me how to beach properly. I should have been reveling in these kinds of views for months. Only I had been so hyper focused on Collin, I let my view turn into nothing but rocks and calculations.

Bro came out and stood next to me. His shoulder rubbed against mine. The sun was making its way toward the horizon, but it was still a good hour or more before sunset.

"This makes up for my missing bag. What do you want to do? We've got twenty-four hours, a beach, and..."

I turned to him as he trailed off. His eyes were dark, and a sexy little quirk turned up the corner of his lips. Oh good, I hadn't been the only one thinking of how to take advantage of our situation.

"Or we could just order room service?" This was a game I knew how to play well.

I turned and began unbuttoning my blouse, letting it trail to the floor behind me as I swayed my hips and sashayed my way into the depths of the room.

I had Bro alone, and nowhere to be, and no one else to have to hide from.

Bro made some undignified noise in his throat.

I smiled. I loved having that kind of power over a man. He thought he was going to be all suave and seduce me, yet here I was, stripping down and stripping away his control at the same time.

By the time I turned around, he was right behind me, his shirt gone, probably on the floor with mine.

"You planned this, didn't you?" His voice was low and thick.

I trailed my fingertip around the lower edge of his collar tattoo. "I don't control the weather. But getting you to a hotel, maybe I had alternative goals than simply being more comfortable than trying to sleep in an airport lounge. Besides, how was I ever going to get you to seduce me in an airport? That wasn't going to happen."

"And the lost luggage?"

"You won't be needing any clothes."

"You don't need to convince me to seduce you," he chuckled.

"No, but clearly you needed an open opportunity. I wasn't sure that was going to happen until we got to Tonga."

My fingers caressed up the thick column of his strong neck. I began trailing teasing little touches along his jaw.

He grabbed my wrist and pressed a kiss to my palm before he scraped his teeth over it, followed by his tongue.

I gasped when he sucked my finger into his mouth and swirled his tongue over and around.

"I'm sorry we've had to hide," he said as he placed delicate kisses along the underside of my arm. He sucked at the fold of my elbow.

I dropped my jaw. I had no idea how sensitive that spot was.

"I can handle a little hiding, but I was beginning to think you had forgotten about what we had started," I confessed.

He lifted me into his arms. I wrapped my arms around his shoulders and twisted my hands into his hair, messing up his half knot, while at the same time I wrapped my legs around his hips.

"I couldn't forget about you, about us, if I wanted to. I was trying to show restraint."

I was making it hard for him to talk as I kept kissing him between words.

"You kept teasing me, showing off those knees of yours," I said between more kisses.

We shifted and he lowered me to the bed. I kept my legs locked around him as he knelt above me. His hands caressed up my middle and over the swell of my breasts. My nipples peaked as he brushed them through the fabric of my bra.

"You like my knees?" He twisted and lifted one of my legs. He caressed the back of my knee.

I squirmed as it tickled.

"I never really paid much attention to knees." He let out a low hum as he dipped his head and licked ever so seductively over my knee. "Yes, I see."

The lick was followed by a gentle scrape of his teeth. "It's a bit boney, I much prefer your softer parts."

My leg fell to the side as he lowered to me and placed his

hot mouth over the fabric of my bra. I arched up to meet him. I almost had his mouth on me.

"Get this off of me," I complained as I twisted out from under him, exposing as much of my back as possible.

Bro reached behind me and deftly unhooked the offending bra. I shoved it from my shoulders and tossed it aside before arcing my back and lifting one breast in offering. Without a word, he sucked my nipple into his hot mouth.

His tongue licked and swirled, teasing my sensitive peak into a conduit of need. Each pull traveled through my body and landed with a greedy need in my core.

"I forgot how good you tasted," he mumbled.

"You're the one who said he was trying to show restraint. That's on you. Oh yes, do that more." I whimpered at a particularly hard suck on my nipple. Or maybe I was melting against the way his hand kneaded at my flesh. He touched my hips, and my soft middle, with as much reverence as he caressed and fondled my breasts.

His skin against mine was like a soft electrical buzz followed by heat. His skin slid against me, soft like suede, hard like granite. The man was a block of solid muscle. He was nothing but contrast and opposites against my body.

I no longer mourned the body I had wanted. How could I when this man worshiped the body I had been gifted, so completely. I shoved those distracting thoughts away. I had to accept I had been put on a particular path for a reason, even if I had thought the destination was different. I liked the end results I was receiving.

Bro's hands skimmed up and under the hem of my travel skirt. He slid a large, firm hand slowly up my thigh, bunching the fabric up until it was barely nothing more than some wadded up belt around my middle.

"I can take this off," I said, trying to squirm the waist-band around to find the button closure.

"Stop." He placed a hand over mine. "Let me. I'm having fun unwrapping you. It's like discovering new and wonderful places."

Braced on my elbows, I watched down my body as he teased his finger across my panties, directly over the slit of my sex. It was a complete turn on to watch him touch me. But my underwear was in the way.

"I wonder what's under here?"

"You forgot so soon?" I teased right back at him. Any further sassiness I might have been ready to spew left my body as he lowered between my legs and did that tooth scraping thing across my panties.

I probably whimpered as I fell back. I lifted my hips in response to the closeness of his mouth to me. I didn't really notice as his fingers dug in, and he pulled the offending garment away from my body.

I was nothing but nerve endings and need. The man knew exactly where all of those nerves resided, and he focused on it with wet licks and focus destroying sucks. I didn't know what to do with my hands. I grabbed his hair, I tore at the skirt still around my middle. I fisted and pulled at the bedding.

My heels pressed down into the bed, and I found the corner of a pillow to sink my teeth into as I vocalized my reactions to Bro's attentions. His tongue was pure delight. He knew exactly how much pressure, and when to leave off with a teasing little lick.

I didn't fool myself into thinking I had any control over my body. His tongue delved into places I had never thought a tongue would go. Then again, he was showing off, and was better than any of the past lovers I could remember. At the moment, there were no other lovers, there was Bro, and only Bro.

My body was his to manipulate and control. If he stopped, I would dissolve into a puddle of tears and longing. I was so close, but I didn't want the fun to be over. With an effort I didn't know I had in me, I twisted my hips away from the magic of his mouth.

"What? Are you okay?" he asked.

I sat up and reached for the button closure of his shorts. The man still had his pants on!

"I want my mouth on you." I demanded.

"Are you sure?"

"I want to suck on you, taste your salt. I want to make you feel as good as you are making me feel," I whined with desperation.

He rolled from the bed and shoved the rest of his clothes from his body. I wiggled out of the skirt that was in danger of cutting me in half.

His cock sprung free. Damn, he was glorious.

I reached for him as he climbed back onto the large king-sized bed. I appreciated a big bed with room to play. And I intended on playing all night long.

I didn't give him time to maneuver before I slid under him, and grabbed his cock. I guided it to my mouth and inhaled him. His knee bumped my shoulder, and I wiggled around until I had one arm positioned around his leg. My fingers bit into the firm muscles of his ass, while the other held his thick cock at the right angle for me.

I wasn't skilled, I was desperate. He filled my mouth and I sucked on him like he was a straw full of my favorite treat.

He said something before his fingers bit into my hips, and his mouth found my sex again.

Yes! My hips lifted to meet him as his tongue did

amazing and magical things to my delicate sex. He was magic between my legs, and I pulled at him with no finesse, and nothing but greed.

He stopped, and tried to pull away from me. "Mancey, you have got to stop."

I didn't want to.

"I'm going to cum if you don't let go."

I was torn. I would swallow him down, but if he went off now, how long before I got to feel him deep inside of me where I wanted him most?

I let go of his cock and gave it a long goodbye lick over the thick vein along the underside.

He shifted, and looked into my face. His smile at that moment was something that I would never forget. He reached forward and brushed his thumb over my lower lip. "You have a greedy mouth, woman."

"Is that bad?" I asked with what breath I had left in my body. I was panting hard with my burning need. I sucked on his thumb. Desperate to have any part of him I could inside of me.

"No woman, it is not bad, not bad at all. Is your pussy that greedy?"

I pushed up on my elbows as he slid from the bed. "I don't know, why don't you come back here and find out."

"I have every intention of doing just that." Bro knelt next to me on the bed. His cock presented and proud.

I reached out and tried to stroke him as he shifted away from me.

He grabbed my hands away from him. "You just like playing with my cock."

"I really do," I admitted, and I reveled in taking him back into my hands and toying with his hardness. His entire body was hard steel covered in suede, his erection doubly so.

I was getting even wetter than I already was with anticipation. Once I had him prepped for action, I fell back and opened my arms and legs for him to come to me, to merge with me.

He did not deny me in that moment. I sighed with satisfaction the moment he slid into me. In that split moment, everything was still and perfect. And then Bro took action. He pounded into me.

I grappled for a grip on his shoulders, and urged him to go harder, faster, deeper with my words and counter thrusts of my hips.

There was no oxygen to scream out his name as he took me beyond what I thought my body could endure. All I could do was hold on tight and ride it out.

Bro did not lose his voice to passion the way I had. He roared with the ferocity of a lion as he was taken over by his own release. He was loud, furious, and almost frightening in the volume he reached.

18

———

Bro was a warm presence at my back when I woke up. I wanted to wake up like this forever. His warmth spread through my body and settled in my chest. I recognized this feeling, this was falling in love. This was everything I had been chasing after.

I rolled and gazed upon his sleeping face. He was so beautiful. Beautiful and strong, and so damned smart, it hurt to think that I had almost missed out because of my single mindedness when it came to going after Collin.

Bro's eyes opened slowly, and then he blinked before shifting his neck so he could see me in focus. "Good morning." His voice was thick and groggy.

His lips were warm as they pressed against mine. He hummed through the kiss.

"It's a very good morning, after a pretty fantastic night. Thank you for that, by the way." I stretched and shifted, so my skin pressed in closer against his big body.

"My pleasure. Pretty sure your pleasure too." He wrapped his arms around me and tugged me in tight.

I ran my leg up the side of his. His skin was smooth and warm. He was perfect.

"I'm going to tell you something, and I don't want you to freak out, or run away," I started. "Even if you don't want to say anything back. I'd rather you just say nothing than run."

"Sounds like you're about to confess you're in love with me. Mancey, that's not something I'd run away from."

"No?"

He shook his head and brought his face right against mine. I couldn't focus on him, he was too close. But I rubbed my nosed against his, and against his cheek. Touching his face with mine.

"No. It feels good, falling in love. I'm glad you are comfortable enough to say it first."

"But I haven't said anything yet," I pointed out.

"Semantics," he grumbled, but he did not move.

"Yes, I'm falling in love with you. So I think I should tell you something else about me, you might not like."

"Why are you telling me everything now?"

Confession one down. Would he be as accepting of the rest?

"I didn't want to start this relationship with any more secrets, lies, or hidden truths."

"Hmm, sounds serious." He brushed my hair away from my face, and I mirrored the action. Only I left my fingers twisted in his hair.

I felt safe wrapped up in his embrace like this. He was holding on to me just as much as I clung to him. He was saying he was staying without using any words.

"I... I died."

"Your accident? Why do you have gaps in your memory?"

"Yeah. But that's not the weird part. I'm not Addison."

He let out a soft chuckle. "The name thing. That's why you go by Mancey now."

"Right. Because I am not Addison. Addison died, and I came back in her body. I can remember being me before I was Addison. I was an actress, a movie star, actually."

"I thought you were a scientist," he pointed out.

I still had him wrapped up in my arms, he wasn't shifting away from me. My heart clenched and relaxed as he stayed with me.

"Exactly. I am a scientist, I was one. Scientific engineer to be more precise, but Addison never was. She never went to college. I don't think her mother would have let her, even if she had been a good student. Addison's parents manipulated her into getting married right out of high school."

Bro's limbs felt stiff all of a sudden. He was still intertwined with me, but his muscles tensed. "You let me believe you were a graduate student."

"I had to come up with something that would let me into Collin's field work."

At the mention of Collin's name, Bro slipped away from me. He rolled to his back, running his hands through his hair, and stared at the ceiling.

I started explaining everything, speaking in rapid fire time. "I saw Collin before I ever became Addison. I followed him around as a ghost before I found a body. And then I became Addison so I could find him again. But how was I to do that? There is no way Addison ever could have come up with the theory that tagged along to Collin's about lava actually communicating. I did that. I found a body, I built the GeoTalker, but then I met you and the thing worked. It actually worked."

"So you're doing all of this for Collin, and his research? What about my research? What about me?"

"That's not what I said," I growled in frustration. He wasn't hearing the words I was saying, but what he wanted to hear. "I said I started because of Collin. But I kept going for me. For the science."

He barked out a harsh laugh as he sat up. "You expect me to believe you were the ghost of a movie star and followed Collin around and never once took my presence into consideration? Your story is as thin as your lies."

I tossed my hands up. How did I make him understand me? "You just don't want to believe. Which is rich coming from you right now. You're claiming that communication with volcanoes has always been your big idea, not Collin's. Fine. It's your brain-child. But how dare you claim sentience from lava and then scoff at the very concept of ghosts or existence on a slightly elevated plane of existence."

Bro shook his head. "Okay, fine. Let's say I believe you that you were a ghost. You're telling me that you were around Collin and never once saw him with me or talk about me?"

I pulled my knees up to my chest and wrapped my arms around them. This was all going so very wrong. Of all the people I had met since being in this body, I had actually thought Bro would have understood. He seemed to get it. Maybe that was just hope and blind lust clouding my judgment.

"I followed Collin around for a good portion of a semester. I don't remember seeing you, ever. And if he mentioned you, I didn't know who you were. Why would I have paid attention to every time he mentioned Dr. Nakamura? Maybe you were doing field work? I don't know."

"Of all the harebrained stories you could come up with." He

was out of the bed and searching the floor for his clothes. He pulled items on as he found them. "The truth would have been nice, not some cockamamie nonsense about being the ghost of some actress. You're not really a grad student? Fine. You had a mental break and can no longer be the person you were, fine. But this ghost story is bullshit. And yes, it's my research, Collin is just along for the ride. Apparently, like you are."

"Bro... Brody, I love you, what are you doing?" The fear I had about telling him the truth coalesced into a hard knot in my stomach. I was going to be sick.

"First of all, I'm not going to Tonga. I can't. You're not well Mancey, Addison. Whatever your name really is. I'm going back to my field work and do some damage control." He was out the door before I could untangle myself from the sheets.

I tried to run after him but ended up on the floor with sheets twined around my legs like some force trying to hold me back. "Bro?"

He was gone by the time I fought the sheets and managed to wrap them around myself before running out the door after him. "Bro!" The door closed on the sheet, stopping me before I became unwrapped.

Nothing. He was gone, and I was alone. I don't know how long I stood in the walkway outside of my room. I was bundled in half a bed sheet, the other half stuck in the door. Tears burned my eyes and the back of my throat.

I had trusted him with everything and he said I was unwell. He might as well have said I was a mental case, the accident had landed me with a serious brain injury, and I had almost managed to fool some people into believing I was someone I wasn't.

But I was me, and Bro had walked away from me.

"Do you need help getting back into your room?" A uniformed maid asked me with deep, kind eyes.

"No, thank you, I've got it." Everything about me felt hollow. I was the void left behind in Bro's departure. He was just gone. I pushed open the door to my room.

Addison was sitting on the couch that looked out over the open deck, and onto the beach when I stepped back inside.

"This is nice. It's about time you did Hawaii properly. Look at that beach, no stupid volcanoes in sight," she said.

I blinked away tears, and wiped at my face. "We're not in Hawaii. This is Fiji. What the fuck are you doing here?" I snarled.

19

———

I dragged my little cart along the dock. The wheels made a steady thump-thump-thump against the wood planking. And when they weren't making a rhythmic sound, they were stuck and causing me grief.

"It smells like dead fish," Addy complained.

"I didn't think you could smell anything," I said over my shoulder. My slight twist caused the oversized backpack to bump into someone, again. I was constantly muttering, "Sorry," over and over. The wharf was a veritable hive of activity, populated with fishing boats and tourists. And it did smell like dead fish and engines. I wasn't sure if the scent was oil or diesel. Something fuel-like that reminded me of train stations and large trucks. The air was cool with the lingering vestiges of early morning, so the smell wasn't nearly as bad as I expected it could be.

"I can't, but it looks like it smells. How can you stand it?" she whined. "Why are we even here? Nobody here looks like us."

"You mean white?" I snapped. "Don't make me lecture you about your narrow-minded, racist upbringing. I thought we agreed, I wasn't going to tolerate that bullshit from you. You're the one who wanted to come along for this ride."

"It's my body."

"You vacated and abandoned the vehicle. Finders keepers."

"That's not what I meant. But I see what you think of me. I meant tourists. There aren't other vacationers out here. Are you sure we aren't lost?" she asked.

For a split second, I felt bad about judging Addison's word choice and jumping to conclusions. I wasn't convinced she was trying hard enough to unlearn the damage Kristin and Bob had done to her cognitive development. I was bound and determined to make her a better person, even if I had no intentions of giving this body back. Who was I fooling? I didn't even know if I could.

"We aren't here to see the sights. We're here for work," I said. I wasn't too worried about anyone thinking I was nutso for talking to myself, the place was so crowded and the noise was so loud, anyone who could have heard me, wouldn't have been paying attention.

"But you said you were taking a break," she whined.

"I did take a break." I had extended my stay in the hotel on the beach in Fiji for almost a whole week. I hadn't wanted to leave in case Bro came back. I didn't know if I could keep going forward on this path without him. After a lot of cajoling, Addy finally agreed to go to the volcano with me. I didn't want to do it alone.

"But we're by the water. Shouldn't we be inland, you know where the volcanoes are?" Addy sounded a bit apprehensive.

"The volcano isn't on this island," I told her.

"Then shouldn't we be headed toward an airport?"

"Why? No. The volcano is an uninhabited island. It

doesn't have an airstrip. I don't even know if it's big enough for one. We're taking a boat."

Addy stopped moving. It took me a moment to realize she was no longer hovering right against my shoulder. I turned around, knocking into someone else with the stupid backpack. Why had I packed all of my notes? I had more notebooks than clothes with me.

"Sorry, sorry," I muttered to anyone who cared or heard me.

I started to reach out and grab her wrist like she was some petulant child and drag her along with me. Someone stepped through her and the projection of her swirled around before reforming. I dropped my arm to my side.

"Come on, I still have to hire a charter to get us there. If we're lucky, we haven't missed all the boats heading out early."

Addy shook her head. Her eyes were wide with panic.

My shoulders slumped under the weight of her fear. What hadn't she told me this time?

"I... I can't. No boats. No boats." She covered her ears and turned and ran away. The sound of her wailing "no boats" on repeat turned into a siren whoop, and then vanished into the noise of the wharf as a screaming seagull.

"Addison!" I called out after her, but she had already vanished. Great, she was afraid of boats. I hoped that wasn't something deep-seated into the muscle memory of this body. I needed to get to the island, and the only way was by boat, several hours in a boat.

I needed to get past the bustle of the crowd and out to where the larger boats were moored. And now it appeared I was well and truly on my own in this. No Addy to run commentary, and no Bro to help with the heavy lifting and negotiating. Not that he ever actually carried anything.

Even without Bro's assistance— he could go wallow in his man-pout for all I cared— I was going to see this research through. I glanced down at the note paper I had. The note was an old one from a previous trip Bro had taken to these islands. The paper was discolored, and almost soft from how often it had been crumpled and folded and refolded. It had made its way into the stack of travel documents at some point.

I reached the area along the wharf where it said I should be able to find either a boat I could charter— I should look for The Albatross Kiss, captained by an old white guy named Drake Albert— if there wasn't a research vessel I could plead my case with.

I found an official looking boat. Okay, maybe a small ship. I don't know how else to describe it, and I didn't know nautical terms. And if Addy knew them, she had just taken off, leaving me completely alone on this adventure. It wasn't as old and beat up as the other boats along the dock. It had a submersible hanging over the back end. And other smaller inflated motorboats strapped to the side. The hull was blue with a bright yellow stripe, and an insignia that looked almost like a government seal, but it said pie. Huh?

I squinted as I tried to focus on the small script. The bobbing of the boat in the water made focusing through my sweat streaked sunglasses a bit tricky. Poseidon Institute of Exploration.

"Hah," I let out a sharp laugh.

It couldn't hurt to ask them. If nothing else, maybe they could steer me in the right direction.

I parked my cart with my equipment and dropped the damned backpack close to their gangplank, which was a wide metal ramp from the dock into the side of the ship, and wandered up the length toward the front to see if I could wave anyone down.

The boat was tall, and I had to crane my neck back to see. If there were people on the deck, they would have to get pretty close to the edge before I was able to see them. It took about ten, maybe fifteen minutes before I saw anyone.

I began waving my arms when a figure appeared, back lit by the sun. "Hello! Hello!"

"Ahoy there," a man shaped figure back lit by the sun leaned over the railing and waved back. "Can I help you?"

"I certainly hope so. I'm in need of a bit of assistance, and information," I called back.

"I'll come down," he said, and then vanished away from the railing.

I meandered toward the gangplank. A long limbed, and very tanned man in a faded t-shirt and the same cargo shorts Bro seemed to prefer jumped from the mid-point and stepped up to me, holding his hand out. He had that deep skin damaged tan that would never fade.

I took his hand and noticed how my skin was so much paler against his than it was against Bro's.

"Dr. Dirk Owens, how can I be of assistance?" the man asked with a noticeable Aussie accent.

"Hi Dr. Owens, my name is Ma- Addison Manchester... Rouche—" It felt weird to say my name like that. And I felt the need to explain myself— "Sorry, I'm in the middle of a name change, I don't know what's legal anymore. That is completely beside the point. I'm so sorry, I'm suddenly flustered now that I've gone off script."

"It's okay, miss, take your time," he chuckled, and laugh lines crinkled around his eyes.

"Call me Mancey. Right. I need to get to Hunga Tonga-Hunga Ha'apai, to conduct some research. My travel companion scarpered on me but left me some notes on either finding a research vessel that might take pity on me, or who to charter a boat from. I'm hoping you might be able to help me out with either?"

Expressions danced across his face. He had to be a horrible poker player, and I now questioned if we were speaking the same language. I mean, yes, he had an Australian accent, but we were both speaking English.

Maybe this was why Bro really abandoned me. My research hypothesis was embarrassing, and he took any excuse other than the real one to not be associated with me once we ran into other scientists.

"Hunga Tonga-Hunga Ha'apai you say?" He rubbed the back of his neck. His face still crinkled in confusion.

"Dr. Brody Nakamura said there was an island that formed, and it would get me close into the caldera of the volcano. I'm studying geological electro pulses to see if they might actually be forms of communication. Can we decipher the pulse patterns? Are they random, or are they signals that could alert us to volcanic or seismic activity?"

Dr. Owens blinked at me some more and then laughed. "That sounds exactly like the kind of thing Bro Nakamura would have been into. You knew him?"

Knew? I didn't think, just because I hadn't spoken to the man in a week, it would qualify for past tense.

"Yeah. I'm here on his recommendation."

Dr. Owens pulled his head back. "You must have only read up through his last paper. Unfortunately, his research was never finished."

"It's on going," I corrected. After all, he was an active boots-on-the-ground volcanologist in Hawaii.

"Unfortunately, I can't help you."

My shoulders sagged. I had a moment of hope that Dr.

Owens was going to say, sure, we'll give you a lift. I looked down, and my gaze landed on his feet. I expected to see boots with thick souls to protect him against the heat of walking on lava formation, but he had on thin plastic flip-flops. His toes were as tanned as the rest of him.

It's a weird detail to have focused on, but I was staring at his toes when I heard him.

"It's good of you to want to continue Dr. Nakamura's work. The scientific community lost a good one when we lost him."

It took a long minute to process what the man was saying. I was caught up in how tan his toes were, and about to get lost in thoughts of him needing a pedicure, when the words started to ricochet around in my skull.

"Lost a good one?" I cut my eyes back up to meet his. What did he mean? Had something happened since Bro stormed out of my hotel room? "What happened?"

Dr. Owens looked at me with a new and improved baffled expression. I must have been taxing the man's what-the-hell response. "I assumed you knew, since you are continuing with some of his work. Isn't that what you said?"

I shook my head. "The hypothesis is all mine."

"But you said you got the idea to come here based on his research..."

I just nodded. What was this man going on about?

"Bro Nakamura, and another geological researcher, along with a charter boat's owner were lost when Hunga Tonga-Hunga Ha'apai blew in 2022. They hadn't made it off the island in time. They were out there taking more samples."

It was my turn to blink and look confused. My jaw dropped open. Bro, Brody Nakamura was dead? I shook my head. "I... I... never encountered that information in my research," I managed to mutter.

The world tilted sideways rather suddenly. I tried to throw my hands out to stabilize myself before I fell over. Bile burned the back of my throat, and my vision turned gray and fuzzy around the edges.

"Are you okay? You should sit down or something. You've gone very pale."

Dr. Owens guided me to the side of the gangplank and helped me down onto my butt

"I'll be right back." He left me on my own.

Bro was dead? Not possible. I had spent twelve glorious hours in bed with him. We had a fight. He left. He walked away from me. He couldn't be dead, he touched me. How could he touch me if he wasn't real?

I stared down at the piece of paper I still clutched in my hand. How did I get this note if Bro was dead?

"Here, have some water," Dr. Owens said as he stepped back out of the ship.

I took the offered cup and drank. It had that staleness of recycled water, but it was wet and cold.

I held up the paper. "Was the name of the lost boat The Albatross Kiss, its captain, Drake Albert?"

Dr. Owens shook his head. "I can't be certain. I'm sorry, I figured you would have known all of this already."

"I should have." I let out a weak chuckle. Damn it. Had Bro ever been real? "What am I supposed to do about my research?"

"What is it you need?" Dr. Owens asked.

"I need to get up close and friendly with an active, or recently active volcano and record its electric pulses."

"Home Reef is currently pretty active," he offered.

"Home Reef is underwater," I countered. "Neither I nor my equipment are capable of underwater research."

"Home Reef has formed a relatively stable island, and at the moment it's in a green zone."

"Green zone?"

"It means we can get close. Maybe even close enough for your needs. Why don't you come aboard and tell me exactly what it is you're doing."

20

———————

I accepted Dr. Owens, Dirk's, invitation onto the P.I.E. vessel, *Cherry Ala Mode*. I found out that the institute had a bit of a sense of humor and all of its boats were named for desserts. They even had a deep sea exploration submersible called *Pizza*. Apparently called that specifically because of Chicago style deep dish pizzas, and it was a deep going vessel. Dirk thought it was hillarious.

"I can't believe you've never had a deep dish pizza. It's the very definition of pizza pie."

I had to admit to never having had one. "I thought all pizzas were just thin slices of dough, sauce, cheese, and toppings."

Dirk rolled his eyes as he seemed to flash back to a culinary memory. "You know food is special when you can remember it years later. Maybe we'll meet up again sometime in the States, and we can go find a Chicago style pizza place. American style pizza is something I've never experienced anywhere else."

"And to think the average American considers pizza an Italian food," I laughed.

Dirk's good humor and warm personality continued once he got past the initial confusion of our meeting. His office was really just a corner in a lab on board the ship. I didn't feel so out dated when I saw I wasn't the only one to record and run calculations on paper first.

When I pointed it out, Dirk explained that ship to shore internet via satellite only worked when they were properly aligned. "Dedicated computer terminals are available, but the uplink of data only occurs at set times. Besides, most of the crew are the hands-on type and have to run calculations on the fly, especially when on a dive. Relying too much on computers can be a hazard."

They lived and worked on a fine line, balancing between the two.

"Of course all the work has to be documented on the computer so it's saved. Note paper and seawater aren't good companions. But most of us find it easier to make our notes, and then transcribe them later," he admitted.

"I was getting grief for doing just that. Of course, my equipment is also old school." I said as I opened the container that housed my GeoTalker and lifted it from the coolers.

"I see," Dirk said.

I brought the heat shielding coolers along. After all, I planned on parking my baby on land that was once lava. It needed a heat shield.

He reached forward, as if to touch some of the elements, but did not actually touch anything.

"That is so steampunk. What is it?" A woman, about my age, said as she stepped into the lab.

"Steampunk?" I asked.

"Yeah, you know antique, futuristic, Jules Vernian, sci-fi," she said as she stepped in close and peered at the GeoTalker like it was a museum piece. I pretty much comprehended the association to Jules Vern. Yes, Victorian era science technologies, steam powered engines.

"I don't know if I'd say steampunk," Dirk started. "Cyber punk?"

And I was lost in their terms again.

"Not techno enough," she said. She stood and reached her hand out across the GeoTalker. "Patty Sommers, interesting toy you have here. What does it do?"

"Mancey," I said. I didn't see any reason to delve back into my weird name situation. A bad habit I did far too often. Especially when it wasn't relevant to the situation.

"Mancey here is following up on some research of a late friend of mine. We have some time, I thought we'd give her a lift out to Home Reef," Dirk said.

I decided that correcting him wasn't worth it. This was my research, and Bro had only pointed me in this direction. It didn't matter until the papers were published who got named where. But Bro's death hit me in the gut. Just thinking about it made my heart hurt, and it was difficult to breathe. But I had to fake my way through this day, especially since Dirk seemed like he might actually help me.

I probably would never be able to publish this anyway. I was a complete fraud when it came to who I was conducting this research for anyway. I pushed aside that very Addison type feeling of insecurity and gave Patty my schpiel.

"I need to record as much time as I can get. The device will record up to twenty-four hours, but I can typically get a reading in less than eight. I need to prove there are patterns worth recording first. And that's why I'm out here. It looks like I've been able to identify unique signaling patterns from activity in Hawaii. I didn't have all this information I needed when I headed out here. But Dr. Owens was kind enough to suggest Home Reef once I gave him the overview of the research."

"So hanging out on volcanoes is what you do for fun?" Patty teased.

I had to admit, I was meeting interesting men this way. "I guess so. This all started from a hypothesis regarding tectonic movement, and a potential way to monitor the caldera under Yellowstone National Park." I had done some reading while on the beach in Fiji. My new-found knowledge of Yellowstone fit into my entire act so effortlessly, I didn't see why I couldn't use it.

"Well, this area is a hot spot for tectonic activity, thus the volcanoes," Dirk offered.

"That is why I'm starting with the volcanoes. They are active and moving in real time, not geological time. But if I can prove the pulse communication, maybe someone will see that as worthwhile to expand into a monitoring situation for the longer term geological activities. I mean, wouldn't it be nice to know if a dormant volcano wakes up before it blows its top and wipes out a population? Or to get people to evacuate before a massive earthquake on one of the faults that run through downtown LA."

"Or Melbourne," Dirk added. "It's got potential."

"I think so. It's still in its baby phases."

"And you think Home Reef is going to help you?" Patty asked.

"The patterns I was able to identify in Hawaii are different enough that I can tell which volcano is being chatty. They are all mostly similar, same magma system. There are some differences, not unlike how siblings are clearly related, but unique?"

I cast my gaze from Dirk to Patty. They both were focused on me and listening with attention.

"Well, I need a volcano outside that system. The other volcanoes I tested in the region were too quiet to be able to tell anything more than they are not providing signals within the testing window. I need to be able to gather signals from other active volcanoes from different magma systems to be able to show that my hypothesis holds water."

Patty and Dirk looked at each other for a long time. It was clear they had some form of other connection— lovers or long time colleagues— where they could somehow communicate just by looking into each other's eyes.

"Are you thinking what I'm thinking?" Patty asked.

Dirk laughed. "That's exactly why I think we can do this for her. We could pack a cooler full of food, and spend the day fishing while Mancey here collects her data."

"You think Strandfield will let us borrow...?"

"I was thinking we tell him after the fact, you know it's easier to ask forgiveness than permission," he said with a twitch of his lips.

"We aren't about to get into trouble, are we?" I asked.

Their response was to laugh.

"Okay, so we were going to get into trouble. As long as I can get my data, and nobody dies in the process, I guess I'm in."

"It might be good to not name us or P.I.E. in the acknowledgements of your paper." Patty said with a little shrug. "You know what I mean?"

21

———

The next morning, before dawn, Patty woke me from the bunk they had let me sleep in.

"Ready?" she asked. Her tones were hushed, and she shushed me when I groaned. Waking up early was for the birds.

She literally walked hunched over and tiptoed through the walkways of the ship as if we were in some spy movie. I didn't bother. No one was going to notice me since everyone was asleep, or they wouldn't care. I was only a temporary guest for the night. Besides, I couldn't carry the GeoTalker and stalk around like some cartoon character.

I was happy to see that Dirk was also not creeping around like a Looney Tune villain. But he was working with quiet swiftness. He packed my things into the back of a lovely speed boat that had been piggy-back docked to the far side of the *Cherry Ala Mode*, so I wouldn't have been able to see it from the dock, even if I had known it was there.

The speed boat was black and red, the colors not coordinating with *Cherry Ala Mode*'s color scheme at all. It had a seating area in the front, a recessed covered cabin area in the middle, with more seating and the captain's steering area in the back. All in all, it was longer and bigger than what I expected. It tickled a memory in the back of my brain. A memory I did not have access to.

Addy wasn't hovering around, so I couldn't ask her if this was one of her memories she so conveniently failed to clue me in on.

"What's this one called? Cherry On Top?" I asked as I crawled down the rope ladder from the *Cherry Ala Mode*.

"It's *The Sea Dervish*," Patty said, still whispering and glaring at me because I was not being quiet.

"That doesn't fit the theme," I pointed out.

"Strandfield considers this to be his private property, thus the clandestine and quiet," she said, emphasizing the last two words.

I made a round O with my mouth as I finally awoke to what our actions were. I hadn't had my morning coffee, and that was the excuse I was going to use for being this clueless this early in the morning. We were borrowing his boat without his permission. Ah, now I understood the trouble we were getting into.

I clamped my lips shut and twisted my fingers next to them, like turning a key. And then I sat down and stayed out of the way.

Dirk and Patty untied *The Sea Dervish* and pushed away from the *Cherry Ala Mode*. Patty actually used a paddle to create distance between the two boats before Dirk turned the engine on.

It was a throaty rumble, no wonder they wanted to get space between them and the other boat before starting her up. The loud rumble would have vibrated through the other ship while they were touching, giving away that we were definitely stealing the boat for the day.

It was a good half hour before dawn lit the horizon, and I had regained my courage to ask questions. The boat bounced over waves as it sped along, leaving the congested water front behind us.

I wobbled as I walked along the narrow space connecting the front area to the back, where Dirk captained the boat.

"How long should this take?" I asked. I had to raise my voice to be heard over the engine.

"Two to three hours, depending on how the sea is," he said.

"So who is Strandfield, and why does he get to have a personal vehicle tied up to your research boat?" I asked.

"He's the boss. And he gets to have his own boat because he rarely goes out with us for long term. He likes to fly into the nearest harbor and spend the day on the water, coming out to us to check in. He typically stays aboard until we come back in. Never really more than a day or two."

"So you had just come back in when I found you?" I asked.

Dirk nodded. "Moored yesterday morning."

"Shouldn't you be back giving reports or something? Shore leave?"

"Shore leave is boring when you would rather have gills," Patty announced, and she appeared out from the covered cabin area. She carried a thermos and several mugs. "Coffee?"

"Fish don't drink coffee," I pointed out.

"I guess it's a good thing we haven't figured out the gill thing, then," Dirk said with a wink as he took the mug from her.

There was definitely something going on between the two of them.

She sat and poured a mug for me. "Why do you think we took the boss's boat and are playing hooky for the day? Reports are boring, but they will get done. Strandfield can deal with the bureaucracy while we have a nice relaxing day."

"It's all in the name of science. He won't get too bothered, and I'll owe him a tank of gas."

"I should probably cover that tank of gas for you, since you're doing this to help be out," I volunteered.

"And I'll let you. I knew Bro, I'm thinking of this as expanding his research. He totally would have been all over talking volcanoes."

My stomach knotted up. I nodded, uncertain what to say. Bro wasn't the one who could communicate with the lava, that was Collin. But Bro certainly supported his friend. Or had he? If Bro wasn't actually alive, how did that change everything I knew about him. How did that change everything I knew about Collin?

"Is there a place I can lay down out of the sun, down there?" I pointed to the cabin. "I'm up way before my alarm and could use a nap before we get there." I also needed a momentary escape. Thinking of Bro made my eyes sting. If I was going to cry, I wanted to be out of sight.

"There's a small bunk. It's not comfortable. You'd be better resting out here," Dirk pointed to the front seating area where I had started this journey.

"Yeah, I don't do sun. I don't tan," I said.

"We're going too fast to put the canopy up," Patty said. "She'll be fine. It's just a little cramped, but it's good for a nap."

I braced myself against the closed in walls of the boat as I stepped down into the cabin area. I found the small birth down below the windows, in an area that had to be under the water level. It was small, and I'd have to climb all the way out if I wanted to turn around, or change my mind. But I was able to curl up, and wrap my arms around a small pillow.

I wanted to cry. How was Bro gone? How had he actually been gone this entire time and I not notice? I wanted a future with that man, and I was only now learning how incredibly impossible that was.

I couldn't go back to seeing Collin the way I first had, that very first time I saw him in Emi's backyard. Yes, Collin was impressive. A block of a man, built more to be an ancient warrior than a college professor. He was stoic and broody, and at one point I had been convinced that was sexy as hell. I had come to learn he was as single-minded and as boring as his sister had accused him of being.

Collin had focus, and determination. He also had a certain pride of heritage. I could never, and would never, force myself into his affections. I wasn't right for him.

I was an annoying outsider. I knew that now. It was his love for the land he was from and its traditions that I found so appealing initially. It was also the exact reason why I should never even try to see him from that same romantic perspective again.

He was no longer attractive that way to me. Knowing that I was not what he would ever want hurt at first. But it made sense. Why would someone who held his traditions so closely even consider looking at a romantic partner from such a vastly different cultural upbringing?

I had wanted to be what Collin would have wanted so badly. But even if I had ended up in the body of a Hawaiian woman, I hadn't grown up with those traditions. I would have looked the part, but not been authentic. My initial feeling for Collin aside, he deserved someone authentic. He deserved something real.

And then there was Bro with his stupid knees he kept flashing at me. Bro didn't care that I came from a different place. He didn't care that my traditions were completely different from his. And it didn't matter what I did, or didn't do, I couldn't have him, no matter how badly I hurt for him.

The boat didn't rock, so much as bounce. Eventually the motion, combined with my lack of sleep from waking up before the sun, lulled me back to sleep.

22

———

I f no one had told me that the island of Home Reef was recently formed as the result of volcanic activity, I would never have known. It looked like a big rock sticking out of the water, and it could have been there forever before we pulled up alongside. The entire island was essentially a wall of cliff face right into the ocean.

There was no beach, it was just a dome sticking out of the water. But it was solid ground. And there were some rocks that we could climb up on. All I needed was a flatish surface to set up and let the GeoTalker do its thing. I may not have been on the main portion of the island, I was still technically on the island, and that was good enough for my research.

"We're going to anchor here and hang out. Do you need anything?" Dirk asked as he jumped from the boat onto the island.

"Just this." I handed out the GeoTalker in its set of stacked coolers. The island was warm, but as far as I could tell it was simply warm because it was a rock under the sun.

I probably wouldn't need to worry about the heat sink aspects of the coolers today.

As Dirk helped me to set up my equipment, Patty put a canopy up over the front sitting area of the boat. I put up my small sun umbrella and began running the GeoTalker through its paces. It needed to be initially calibrated after all the jostling it took during the travel to get it to this location.

The GeoTalker behaved, thanks to good engineering, if I say so myself. The calibration only took a short amount of time, and then the GeoTalker was recording data.

"How much time do you think we can spend out here?" I asked. With some help, I got back on the boat and parked myself under the canopy.

"How much time do you need?"

I twisted and looked at the lone cooler sitting on the rock. It looked completely random and out of place.

"I could use as much data as possible. But it was a long ride to get out here, I don't want to keep you out any later than you want to be. I certainly don't want you to get in any additional trouble with your boss for having his boat out all day."

"Strandfield will have his shorts in the same bunch if we have the boat for one hour or five. Don't worry about that. But I'd rather get in before sunset. That way you can get set up for the evening, and not get trapped with us on the Cherry for another night."

I nodded, it all sounded logical. The plan we ended up with gave me several hours of data recording.

Since there was nothing for me to do while the GeoTalker did its thing, I stared out at the water and chatted with Patty and Dirk.

They had learned all about my research the previous day, today was my turn to learn about the research they did with P.I.E. Patty focused on coral growth patterns and ways to help reestablish colonies that were being impacted by global warming and increased ocean temperatures. The work she did around volcanic areas helped to gain understanding of how ocean life thrived in a variety of temperate zones.

There were lifeforms that needed the warmer waters. She worked in conjunction with the researchers who studied what the shift in the floral and fauna make up of the undersea world would be as temperatures continued to rise.

About then is when both she and Dirk started waxing poetically about different dives they had been on.

"You should get certified. It's a completely different world under there."

I laughed and shook my head. "I'm good with swimming, but I don't think going down into the depths is something I would be comfortable with."

After all, I was still only learning about this body. I knew that Addison had drowned, and something about being under the weight of all that water felt too much like claustrophobia trying to prickle my nerves.

The rest of the day felt like a calm relaxing day on a boat, taking in the sea air, trying not to think too hard about the situation I was in with Bro, or most likely, without him.

The GeoTalker did its job, and at the end of the day I wasn't even subjected to having to witness the fallout with Strandfield.

"I think it's best we just drop you off here," Dirk said as he pulled the boat alongside a public access dock.

"Won't your boss maybe take it easier on you if I explain?" I said, all while unloading my equipment and bags.

"It won't make a difference. And this way you don't have

to get involved in a long-drawn-out conflict that's been going on between the two of them for years," Patty said as she helped me to move my stuff.

It was as if they had been the ones who were ghosts, as they pulled away from the dock, leaving me waving after them. No documentation that they ferried me out to the island, no mention of thanks when or if I published the research. And no consequences of being an accessory to their delinquency.

"Wait, I forgot…" I began to call out after them. They never would have heard me over the engine. We had forgotten to have me cover the cost of a tank of gas for *The Sea Dervish*. I guess I could just make an anonymous donation to the institute.

I stood and watched them for a bit. The sun was low but not yet setting. I had plenty of time to find a taxi and get to a hotel for the night.

The air inside the hotel was cool, yet humid. It wasn't the top of the line, then again, I wasn't paying for anything much more than a clean and secure room for the night. In the morning I'd be back on an airplane returning to Hawaii. For what?

To return to my research group? They weren't my group, and the reality of it was, I was barely tolerated. The grand plan to worm my way into Collin's affections had landed me in deep with Bro, and yet, the entire time I had been so completely unaware that he wasn't really there.

Either I had sucked as a ghost, or he wasn't aware that he really was one. It didn't matter. I stared at the cooler that housed the GeoTalker. Did my research even matter?

What was the point anymore? It was early, but I was tired. I decided to ignore it all and just go to bed.

A loud knock, more of a banging, sounded against my door.

"Miss Rouche?" There was a rumble of voices. "Mancey?" The voice was commanding and completely unfamiliar.

"Hold on," I said with a mouth full of toothpaste. I rinsed and spit, and rushed to find a shirt to put on over my underwear. "Give me a second, please."

I grabbed my sleep shirt and pulled it on over myself before opening the door. "Can I help you?"

An average sized man stood in front of me with a stern expression on his face. He was a bit of an older guy, with a short sandy beard that had once been red, and a head full of the same red hair shot through with more white. Behind him towered Dr. Owens.

"Dirk? How did you find me?" And then I realized who the stern man was. "You must be Mr. Strandfield. I can explain."

He stepped into my room uninvited. Dirk hovered in the hallway. "That's Captain Strandfield, and I dare say I think you should. Because if I understand what Dr.s Owens and Sommers told me, you are in need of our assistance."

I backed up in a bit of shock. I was expecting a reprimand from this man who looked like he spent years as a school principal and knew how to scold. "Wait, help me?"

"You need some underwater research conducted, and we do underwater. We're the Poseidon Institute of Exploration, it's what we do."

I gaped at the man before turning my confused gaze to Dirk. He just shrugged.

I started laughing. "I thought this was going to be about not paying for a tank of gas."

23

—————

The next morning, I was back on *Cherry Ala Mode*. And instead of Dirk and Patty poking at my vintage equipment, I had the attention of an entire, though small, scientific and engineering team.

Strandfield loved the concept of the natural world communicating in ways we didn't understand. As he pointed out, everything was energy and communication was patterned energy, so then why not? All we needed to do was decipher the code.

Apparently, he had a little side project that was currently attempting to learn whale song. He was convinced that dolphins and whales were "speaking" the same languages but at different frequencies. Whale song needed to carry far distances, while dolphins were communicating with those in their local pod.

I think Patty summed it up best for me. "You know how grandparents and old people talk slow, and middle schoolers talk like they don't need to breathe?"

I nodded.

"I think it's like that. But we still don't know what they are saying."

"Curious choices you've made here," Strandfield said as he and his top engineer, Gunner some-last-name-I couldn't-understand-let-alone-pronounce, examined the GeoTalker.

"What made you even think about using vacuum tubes?" Gunner asked with a slight accent I couldn't place.

I was a little bit in love with how everyone on board this ship had come from someplace different. And not in the least intimidated that they were taking me seriously and inviting me to join them, even if for a brief moment of time.

I shrugged. "It's what I was used to." I didn't want to lie to these lovely people who were out of the goodness of their hearts, sense of scientific exploration, and funding from their own pockets taking me under their wing— I was fully prepared to self-fund, but that hadn't come up yet.

"I, uh, used to make simple circuit boards with this kind of stuff. It was always lying around in my grandfather's old workshop." Truth. "And when I stumbled on all the pieces at a flea market, I thought why not." I wasn't going to tell them I made it to look like a prop more so than to actually be functional. I couldn't help it if I made something that actually worked.

"I wonder if there is something in the analog tech that makes tracking and recording more possible than digitally?" I think Gunner was mostly thinking out loud at this point.

He lifted it from the table it was on and took it across the lab before hooking a set of electrode clips to it. I reached out as he walked away with my baby.

Strandfield eased my arm down. "Don't worry, he just wants to see how it works. That way, we can duplicate your effort and create a GeoTalker we can take underwater."

"Yeah, I don't think even with proper housing, this one will handle getting wet," I admitted.

"Your cooler system is clever."

"I wish I could take credit for that. The research team I was piggybacking off of in Hawaii used them as make-shift heat shields. I just copied their efforts, and used their cast off coolers. I was trying to figure out how to fabricate a fiberglass box without a workshop when—" I had to gulp and stop myself from saying it was Bro who had given me the idea— "one of the graduate students pointed out I was spinning my wheels. Why not do what they had done?"

I pointed to some of the melted bits. "That happened when the ground under my feet gave way to lava, and it tried to eat my equipment. I was saved by one of the professors out there with us."

My gut clenched. One of... turns out, Collin really had been the only professor out there. Bro's presence might have been there, but his body certainly wasn't.

"You really hadn't built this for extremes, had you?" Dirk asked.

"Extremes?" I asked. "Oh, right, you mean the lava, or going underwater. No I hadn't. To be honest, I hadn't taken into account all the places I might need to use it. A bit of a scientific method fail for me there."

"Sometimes we miss the obvious. I probably would have missed the heat situation as well."

"But you would have made it waterproof," Strandfield interjected.

"Definitely waterproof." Dirk stood on the other side of the room with his hands on the backs of his hips as he watched Gunner run some telemetry on the GeoTalker. The man was tall and skinny, and the way his arms stuck out behind him, he looked somewhat like a chicken.

It turned out he was a very smart chicken. And so was Gunner. They all were. Patty scrounged some spare parts on board, and an interesting off boat excursion into town later, the team was able to wrangle up enough parts for me to start building a second GeoTalker. Only this new one had to be slightly more compact so that it could fit into a pre-existing set of waterproof housings they already had on board.

It all happened so fast. And almost before I realized what was happening, I was a part of *Cherry Ala Mode's* research team. Before the ship was underway, and there was internet access, I emailed Mark at the campgrounds letting him know I wouldn't be back for several weeks, and to please box my belongings up. Not that I had much, some clothes and my bike. I'd cover any of the storage costs, but there was no reason for me to occupy one of the cabins when I wasn't going to be around.

I was going to live on a research ship for the next three to six weeks, and these crazy, wonderful people were going to help me record data from underground volcanoes. After Mark, I contacted Sadie.

Where have you been? Everyone here thought you might have gotten hurt or something. You disappeared.

She responded almost immediately after I emailed letting her know I wouldn't be around for a while.

You knew we were leaving. I typed. Guilt hit me as I realized I had trusted Bro to let Collin and the others know we were headed out for some extensive field work.

I hit the delete key, backing out of that sentence. At least I hadn't hit send.

Sorry, thought I mentioned it. Needed volcanic activity away from Hawaii. It's turned into an amazing opportunity. I've been adopted by the Poseidon Institute of Exploration for the next few weeks. They are going to help me take this underwater! I liked Sadie and felt like a heel for having left her in the lurch. I hit send on the email.

How much different would this entire situation be if Bro was alive? Sadie and the others back in Hawaii would have known I was gone, and I'd be standing in the wings as Bro and his colleagues on the boat got caught up. Or would this opportunity to become part of the crew on board *Cherry Ala Mode* have even been a possibility?

24

If everything Dirk had said over the course of the past several weeks was true. I was going to need to reference Dr. Brody Nakamura in my paper. And, yes, I was going to publish.

With the help of P.I.E., my research grew and took on a scope I never could have imagined. After all, I had made it up to be closer to Collin. I didn't have to be a grad student, or a doctor with a Ph.D in anything to conduct research and publish. Of course, having credentials helped, but my credentials were now officially as a member of PIE. Their name was sweet on so many levels, including the reputation they held within the scientific community.

That meant I was publishing my findings. To do it properly, I had to document and acknowledge those who came before. And that meant I was going to have to spend quality time with a computer doing research. After all, I wasn't the first person to theorize that the natural world was attempting to communicate with us, we were just too wrapped up in hubris to realize we weren't the only creatures or things with language.

Research on that level wasn't easy on a boat out in the middle of the ocean. I expected that I was going to be sighting Bro's as well as Collin's work in the field. After all, it was Collin's affinity to having a connection with lava that made me think of this not-so-stupid theory. I honestly never expected anything to come of it. I just needed a hypothesis to be plausible enough that Collin wouldn't boot me from his field lab. I didn't realize Bro was in on it until I began working with him.

"Any news on a satellite uplink this morning?" I asked as I staggered into the workroom. My staggering had less to do with sea legs and more to do with my standard morning lack of function.

Mornings started early aboard *Cherry Ala Mode*. We worked when the sun was up and rested when it was down.

Life on the high seas was anything but boring. I found that if the boat was properly stocked, it could handle being away from land for a solid six weeks at a time. More if we really prepared for it. The need for communication access, not just ship to shore communications, but internet and online research library access dictated how frequently we tended to dock. Land typically meant better online access.

There was that one time we sailed around in tandem with a US Navy aircraft carrier for almost a week just so we could borrow some bandwidth. And there was another time we moored alongside a party barge— a container ship some rich playboy turned into a personal floating nightclub, complete with DJs and full catering. Billionaires and their toys, this guy had a satellite that was synchronized to his location, and not the other way around. I bet NASA hated him.

We loved him. We had open access to the internet, and

some late night parties with really expensive booze. No matter what anyone might say, scientists aren't boring, they are focused and that tends to separate them from the party. But when the party is a requirement of friendly satellite access, we hold our own.

Depending on our location, and the weather, we traveled with full access to all the water sports a person could think of. Diving, skiing, surfing, and of course, swimming. Something about swimming in the middle of the ocean was both thrilling and terrifying. I just ignored the hind part of my brain that wanted to make it into something 'oh so scary, there are monsters in the deep.'

Those monsters were exactly what most of the crew was there to find and study. They would have been more than thrilled if the kraken or Captain Nemo had surfaced during one of our recreational moments. And I learned to dive. Bro would have been impressed.

"We are expected to have a signal around oh nine hundred if Gunner's telemetry is correct."

Gunner was never wrong.

I had a few hours before I would start looking for anything and everything Dr. Brody Nakamura ever wrote on volcanic activity. I also needed Collin's work. I started making notes in one of my perpetual notebooks of what I was looking for.

"How much time are they going to give us today?" I asked. Nothing was more frustrating than getting deep into an internet research project to have access yanked away because the boat and the satellites were traveling in opposite directions.

Dirk shrugged. "I was promised a couple of hours, but wasn't told anything firm."

I grumbled low in my throat. I needed a good solid week of access to documents to round out this section of my paper. "I might need shore leave to finish this up."

"No need for that," Gunner announced as he walked into the workroom. "We will have an uplink for three hours today, and by tomorrow afternoon we will be mooring alongside a vessel from SAS Ocean Phoenix at the Western Garbage Patch, and some other group."

"That's happening tomorrow?" Dirk sounded giddy. "I thought we were still waiting for confirmation."

"Confirmation came in, five minutes ago. We change course after our uplink time is over."

"I can see how that's good for you." Dirk and Patty were both heavily involved in conservation aspects of their research. "But how does that help me? I need to hit a library database."

"The French have arranged for a satellite parked in geosynchronous orbit for the duration of this little confab," Gunner said.

Dirk laughed. "You'll be able to do all the research you need while us big kids are talking trash."

And I did. There was an international gathering of scientists, both young and old, discussing current clean up efforts and how they could improve them while we floated next to a giant plastic island of ocean litter. And while they did that, I did a deep dive on Brody Nakamura and Collin Paulo.

I had it all wrong. It had never been Collin's big idea. I had been Bro's all along. Collin's research on communications from lava leaned heavily on Bro's original ideas. Not the other way around.

Bro had been a long time family friend of the Paulo's. He

had been the friend who saw young Collin try to protect lava from a sudden downpour, and took that one small interaction and turned it into a short-lived comic. B. Nakamura was the signature on all the Pele and Pete drawings. I had looked right at that drawing and not even noticed the scribble of a signature or made the connection.

The satellite connection was slow but consistent. I was able to locate the information I needed. I had copies of both Bro's and Collin's theses, and other articles they had published. I downloaded everything I could find to read offline. I knew how precious a commodity this access time was. I wasn't going to waste it reviewing papers that I didn't need an internet connection to read.

While the trash talks continued, I had time to do a little additional research of my own. I wanted to find out everything I could about Bro. I knew I hadn't made him up in my mind. But what details were real? What had he really looked like? If Bro had been the driving force behind Collin's choices, just how old was he? I needed to see for myself. That's when I found the photos.

Looking at pictures of Bro's life stabbed into my chest. The pain was sharp and unexpected. I struggled to breathe around the pain. How could I hurt this much for someone who had been an apparition? How was it that I could see and touch him?

The Bro I knew and loved looked like what the man had back in the late nineteen eighties. He had been close to seventy when he was killed. I downloaded and printed off my favorite picture. One where he was dressed for a performance, and his smile reached out through the image and clutched at my heart.

No wonder Collin was so cranky and broody. He had lost

a long term mentor and friend. That kind of loss had to cut deep. I hurt every day I wasn't with Bro, and I had only known him for a few weeks in comparison. This new realization didn't change my feelings for Collin. I think I just finally understood him a bit better. He was never mine to pursue, it just took me a minute to clue in.

25

"Mancey, can I speak with you a moment?" Captain Strandfield asked.

"Of course." I got up from my work station. He had joined the crew a few days earlier. We were close to New Zealand at the moment. Anytime we were relatively close to land, Captain Strandfield showed up.

Technically, I learned he should have been called Admiral since he was in charge of multiple boats, but he never reached that status in the Navy, so he preferred the title Captain. I wasn't going to argue nautical terms with the man. I had been an unofficial crew member for a couple of months, he had spent his life at sea.

I followed him down the narrow hall to his office.

"Did you have comments on my paper?" I had submitted a final draft to him and was waiting to hear his thoughts before I hit send on the final publication.

"I did, I'll get those emailed back to you. So far from what I've read it looks good, but that's not what this is about."

Those little nerves in my lower abdomen, the ones that said I was in trouble, jumped into action.

"I understand you are, well, how do I put this? Not a traditional scientist."

Crap. He had found out. I bit my lip. Hopefully he wouldn't put me off the ship someplace completely remote. International travel was a pain in my butt. I didn't want to navigate it from the middle of the Pacific.

"I guess that's one way of putting it," I said.

"We embrace initiative at PIE, but want to hear from you directly."

"What? That I'm not a graduate student? I think the fact that I haven't needed to report to an academic advisor has been pretty obvious by now." I let out a heavy breath.

Strandfield nodded.

"But the research is real," I added.

"And the funding?"

I shook my head. "No grant behind this either. You remember my accident, right?"

He nodded. I had to confess certain things from my past, like why I didn't have a valid driver's license. Not that that prevented me from driving in some locations, but in others, I really needed that documentation.

"Massive, and I mean massive insurance payout."

"You've been self-funding this entire time?" he asked.

I nodded and chewed on my lip. I was in so much trouble.

"Now that we've cleared that up. I can offer you a position with PIE knowing all of that."

"Wait what?" I had expected him to say it was time to pack up and leave. "You're offering me a job?"

"You have proven to have a sharp scientific mind, and your track record aboard this ship proves that you are a real crew member. Assisting other's with their research, pitching in when and where it's needed. I want your brain and enthusiasm to be a permanent member."

My jaw fell open, and I gaped at the man like a fish out of water.

"Are you serious?"

He nodded. I wanted to throw my arms around him and hug him, but to be honest, he scared me a little bit. There was something very intimidating about his averageness. It hid something, I was pretty sure it was something ruthless and dangerous. I was glad to be on his good side.

"There are a few issues that will need to be cleared up," he said.

I nodded. I knew what he meant. I needed to be cleared for a driver's license, and I needed to get one.

"We'll be docking in Sydney in a week," he started.

"I'll see if I can get an appointment with a doctor, and have them clear me medically," I volunteered.

"Good, good, you'll also need to arrange for your college transcripts."

I opened my mouth to speak, but he held his hand up, effectively shutting me up.

"It doesn't matter if you don't really have a graduate degree—"

"Does it matter if I have a degree at all?" I cut him off.

Strandfield raised his brows and blinked a few times. "Well, that is going to make a bit of a difference. While we're in Sydney, why don't you see if you can locate a correspondence school, and get that degree underway."

"You really don't care?" I asked, stunned.

"Of course, it would be better if you already had a degree. You're a good fit, Mancey. We want you here. We'll just have to give you a different job title until you can produce transcripts showing you have a degree. Preferably in a science field."

I really wanted to squeal and dance with joy. Everything was working out better than I had thought it could. After Bro abandoned me I felt so completely lost, and here I was feeling very found and in a place where I belonged.

About two months later, there were still things I needed to clear up from Addison's life so I could truly be me. *Cherry Ala Mode* was back in the United States, and I had some work to get done that I couldn't do on a boat.

Strandfield waited for me at the bottom of the gang-plank. "Are you certain about this?"

I gave him a small smile as I shook my head. "I went from one extreme to another. I literally skipped out on my hosts to run away with your group. I love being with PIE, but I need to wrap things up here."

"But six weeks?" he asked.

I shrugged. "I don't know what kind of a mess I may have left behind. And six weeks gives you enough time to complete a standard run while I figure out what's going on in my life. I don't want to be a burden because I don't know how long any of this is going to take."

He slowly nodded. "Take the time you need. If you decide you no longer want to work with us, don't be afraid to let us know."

"I promise you it's not that. I fully plan on being back on board the Cherry in six weeks."

"We'll see you in six weeks on Oahu."

I waved as I walked away from the docked ship on wobbly legs. I made my way down the wharf and out to where I could catch a cab. After months of adjusting to sea legs, land legs made me feel as if I were lurching around. No wonder that Jack Sparrow character was always staggering about as if he were drunk. He didn't have his land legs back.

I had found my place in the world with the Poseidon Institute of Exploration. I could be Manchester "Mancey" Amador, without any of Addison Rouche's baggage. After what felt like an infinite amount of floundering over the name, I decided to go back to a combination of my pre-stage name and the name I had come to think of myself as. I was finally able to commit without having Addy hovering over my shoulder.

I finally filed for my name change during one of our furloughs state side. It went through while we were somewhere in the Pacific, and everyone I knew already called me Mancey.

I took a cab to a hotel, where I spent a day making calls and arranging to get my items from storage at the campgrounds. I could have gone straight to the campgrounds and got a cabin, I had everything I needed there. But hotel beds were much more comfortable than the one in the cabin.

I spent my first day back on the island tracking down all the arrangements I thought I would need during my break. There were items to collect and appointments to be made. I needed to pick my boxes up from the campgrounds, run some errands, and then head to the mainland before flying back for a visit to Emi and to spend a few weeks on Maui. After that, I would find my way over to Honolulu, and rejoin the PIE crew.

And while on Oahu, I needed to visit Collin, who was back in the classroom lecturing. He deserved to see the results of my research. I also owed him a huge apology for forcing my way into his field work, and then leaving without any formal notification. An email to one of his students had not been very professional of me.

"I don't think this will take very long," I said to the driver as I slid out of the car. "I need to pick up a few boxes, and then I'll be ready to go."

My buddy Mark no longer worked for the campgrounds, but the person over the phone knew exactly who I was and where my things were. I wasn't sure what to do with the bike, maybe they could keep it and have an official campgrounds bike.

I turned to run up the steps but was stopped by the apparition of a woman sitting on the top step.

'Where the hell have you been?' Addy sneered at me.

I had to blink a few times. "I thought you were dead," I said aloud.

She narrowed a glare at me. Her face pinched, her lips curled up in derision. She shook at me aggressively.

'I mean, that you moved on.' I stepped past her and into the small office. "Hi, I think I spoke to you yesterday. I'm picking up a couple of boxes you've been storing for me."

I waited until the lady behind the counter wandered off into a back room before addressing Addy again.

"Have you been waiting here this whole time?" I asked in hushed tones.

"I didn't know where else to go. I figured you'd come back at some point," Addy said. Her voice was thick with annoyance.

"Well you are the one who stuck your fingers in your ears and ran away leaving me alone in a foreign country. What was I supposed to do?" I asked with almost as much animosity.

"You were about to get on a boat." Addy flared her nostrils and pouted when the office lady came back out and deposited my boxes on the counter. Addy knew I didn't like having conversations with her when other people were around. It was awkward.

I paid the balance owed for storing my belongings, told the lady I didn't care what she did with the bike, and left. I hauled the boxes, one at a time, out to the car. "Can we talk about this later?" I hissed at Addy as I carried the first box out.

She continued to pout in the back of the car as I had the driver take me around Hilo.

'I think you owe me an apology,' Addy tried to engage while we were in the car.

I simply glared at her before shaking my head.

'Aren't you going to talk to me?' she demanded as I donated half the items I would never need again, such as the bedding at the local Goodwill.

"You know I won't engage when people can overhear." I said through clenched teeth.

After that, we headed to a strip mall with one of those discount department stores so I could get a new suitcase to pack the rest of my things into. It wasn't until I was checked into the airport and waiting for the flight to Maui that I felt comfortable conversing with my invisible companion.

Addy sat in mopey silence, giving me the cold shoulder. She didn't seem to understand that I was doing just fine without her.

"I take it the past few months have been hard for you?" I asked in low tones. "Couldn't you find me?"

When I had been in her situation, I didn't seem to have any problems finding people. I was able to buzz around Collin and get back to Emi, and they had been living on different islands at the time.

"You were on a boat," she said.

"You said something like that earlier. So what?"

"A boat, Mancey! You know I can't do boats." She was yelling. It was a good thing no one but me could hear her.

"How would I know that? Addison, you seem to think I know everything about you. I don't. You're almost as bad as your mother. No, you're worse."

"Don't compare me to my mother!"

"Why not? She can't seem to remember from one conversation to the next that I don't have any memories from your life. And you won't even tell me the important parts. How am I supposed to know you don't like boats, if the second we get near one you run off wailing? Do I need to remind you how you abandoned me to fend for myself against Tyler's first wife?" It took a lot of self-control to not yell back at the moment.

"I couldn't face her. She hates me," Addy said weakly.

I looked up as my flight was announced. With an exasperated sigh, I pushed to my feet and hitched my bag more firmly onto my shoulder.

"She made that pretty clear. But you could have at least warned me who she was. I had to navigate that entire encounter solo. I didn't live your life Addy, I haven't been given your memories. I found out the hard way that your body isn't a fan of flying. That's something you might have warned me about."

"But you're getting on a plane anyway," she pointed out.

"I am, because I'm not afraid of flying, and I'm the one behind the wheel right now. We can pick this up when we land."

I handed the flight attendant my ticket at the gate.

"I thought we were going to Maui?" Addy asked. "This flight is going to Idaho. Why are you going home?"

26

I ignored Addy the entire flight. We were packed in close quarters with cranky vacationing families returning home on a budget friendly airline. I slept most of the way. I didn't want to be headed back to Moscow, but I had an overdue doctor's appointment. I needed this body to get cleared for things such as driving, and scuba diving— even though I was already doing these things. It turned out a lot of the places PIE made land didn't care if I had a license or not. All that mattered was I could drive a stick.

But larger countries tended to be a little fussy about that legality. The doctor that had treated me immediately following the incident had forwarded all of my records to the Rouche's family doctor in Moscow. And he was the one who could officially clear me.

I had tried to have a doctor in Sydney give me an okay. But the second he found out I had been dead for a couple of minutes, he said that wasn't something he was willing to do. But hey, I looked great for a dead lady.

If I was going to officially leave Addison Rouche behind, that meant I had to close her case on this health issue with clearance and dismissal of treatment. And that meant I had to visit Dr. Oswald in Moscow.

"We are not here for old home week," I told Addy. "I'm here for an appointment, and then I'm right back on a plane."

"I don't get to see mom?"

"You can flit off and visit whomever you please. I will not be seeing your mother," I let her know.

There were no calls to check in on Addison's family. They had no way of knowing I was even in the state. I had rather effectively cut ties. It was easy when they were people I didn't know, and didn't want to know.

As far as I was concerned, Moscow was an in and out operation. I'd take the shuttle bus in, stay the night, see the doctor and scamper out of there just as quickly on an evening bus back to the airport. At least that's what was supposed to happen. Everything was fine until I arrived at Dr. Oswald's office.

"Addison! I haven't seen you in so long," the receptionist gushed at me. When I say gushed, I mean she oozed with the enthusiasm of a fan from my Hollywood days.

I returned her grin and cast a quick glance over my shoulder. Where the hell was Addy when I needed her. This was exactly the kind of situation I had been complaining about. This woman thought I knew her. I did not.

"Well, I've not been to the doctor for a while. I've been out of town."

She made some kind of grumble in her throat. "You know, that's not what I'm talking about. I've only worked for Dr. Oswald for, like, three months now. I heard you left Tyler."

"That's been a while. And you also probably heard I had an accident, and have suffered some memory issues..." I shook my head trying to let her know I didn't have a clue who she was. Since this was a doctor's office and not retail, she wasn't wearing a name tag.

She flapped her hand in a dismissive wave. "Pish, we all know that's so you don't have to deal with Tyler and his nonsense."

Fortunately, someone needed her attention to check out, so I was saved from any additional conversation.

When the nurse called my name, the other lady told me to tell my mom 'hi,' for her.

"I'll tell someone you said hi," I muttered.

When I had made the appointment, I fully expected to be on my own, no Addison. But now that she was back breathing down my neck, the least she could do was be helpful. But she couldn't even do this. I shouldn't complain, after all, I did send her on her merry way.

Maybe she would decide that haunting me wasn't nearly as much fun as hanging around her hometown. She could happily haunt away here for the rest of her eternity if that's what she wanted. If she had plans on hanging out with me, I was going to need her to pick up some slack with the memory issues.

The visit with Dr. Oswald went about as expected. He shined a light in my eyes, up my nose, and in my ears. He listened to my breathing. And then he asked me questions I didn't have a clue about.

But I was Manchester Ardmor, not Addy Rouche, and I wasn't going to let him strong-arm me into a wait and see situation.

"Look, I can remember everything from the point of regaining consciousness. I've taken on a challenging and exciting job with an international ocean conservation organization. I know how computers work. And honestly, I've been driving jeeps in a few different rain forests over the past six months without a license."

"If you can do all of that without me telling you, you're healthy, why come to me now?" the doctor asked.

"My boss won't let me get officially scuba certified, or take me for a driver's license without official medical clearance. And before you ask why I came back here and didn't just go to some other local doc, I did. And he officially wouldn't do anything since he hadn't seen my medical history, while being aware of what it was."

"You could have just requested your records." Dr. Oswald crossed his arms.

I nodded. He was right. I don't think any of us had thought that through. "I didn't have enough time. We were only in Sydney for forty-eight hours. I'm on temporary leave, partially so that I can get this taken care of."

"Fine, I'll write it up now. Come with me."

I followed him to his office. Where he typed something up on his computer, and then handed me a print-out.

"How's that?"

I scanned over the words. It was ninety-nine percent perfect. I leaned over his desk and pointed to the part with the names. "Can you indicate here that my name was Addison Rouche, but now is Manchester Amador. I had it changed. You know, redefining myself since the accident."

He didn't say much, mostly grunted before fixing the name per my request.

With my newly minted medical clearance folded and tucked safely inside my bag, I shook his hand. "Thank you, Dr. Oswald. This helps a lot."

"With the new you?" he asked.

"The new me, and getting on with living." I didn't need

to go into all the deeper meaning of it all. That's what Addison's therapist had been for.

I stepped out of his office and all the air left my lungs. It felt like a sucker punch to the solar plexus to hear that woman screech at me.

"Addison Tiffany Rouche!" Kristen said the entire name as if she were preparing to ground me.

And standing right behind her mother was the wavering form of Addy.

"Surprise!" the receptionist called out.

"What the fuck? Why is she here?" I directed my first question to the receptionist.

"It's a total coincidence, when your mom called to schedule an appointment, I told her you were in the office today. Isn't this just great?"

I was done playing nice. I pointed at her with an accusatory pointer finger. "I don't know who the fuck you think you are." I then swirled my finger around, indicating the office. "But this is a clear violation of patient rights. You had no business telling this woman I was here."

I turned my attention to Addison, who as far as anyone else was concerned wasn't there. "You wanted to see your mother so badly, well there she is. She is all yours."

I strode right past them all and out of the office. Unfortunately, I did not have a car waiting to pick me up, so my getaway was thwarted.

"How dare you walk away from me." Kristin was hot on my heels.

"Easily, like this," I said as I continued to walk through the parking lot. I had no idea where I was headed, I just needed to get away.

"You don't even have the decency to call to let us know

you are in town. I had to find out from Kathy at Dr. Oswald's office."

I stopped to turn and face her. "Maybe because I didn't want you to know I was here, Kristen."

"Mom, I'm mom. I keep telling you."

"And I keep telling you that I don't remember you. You cannot force a relationship on someone who doesn't want it."

"We'll see about that," Kristin snapped as she pulled out her phone and called someone.

'But what if I want it?' Addy asked.

I turned to face the space she was occupying. "Then stay."

'I want my body back.'

I tossed up my hands. This was all so frustrating. "I don't know how to do that. You abandoned me for months at the beginning, and you keep leaving important parts of your life out. Things that would have made being you easier. Why do you want back so badly? Your parents have never been nice to you. She's probably calling the cops or an ambulance to get a mental health hold on us right now."

'Mom wouldn't do that,' Addison sniffled.

"The hell she wouldn't. She's been emotionally abusing you your entire life. She set you up with a married man almost twice your age, and that's the one I do know about. She's called you dumb to my face, meaning she thought she was telling you that you were dumb. Come on, Addison, this isn't healthy."

'It's my life,' she said.

"Not anymore. You can stay here for all I care, but I'm not doing this. I can't pretend to be you for these people, and I won't." I continued to walk. There were some shops about two blocks away, once I got past the medical office buildings and across the street from the grocery store. I'd get a ride from there.

'*My mom loves me,*' Addison cried.

I paused. "I'm sorry that's how she loves you. Love shouldn't hurt."

A big black pick up screeched to a stop in front of me. I was confused as everything unfolded around me. Kristen was yelling, and Addison started wailing like a banshee.

My brow knit together as Bob climbed out of the passenger side. This wasn't his truck. I turned and saw Tyler climb down from the driver's side.

"Well fuck."

"You're going home with us," Kristin announced.

"No!" Addison's cry ricocheted off the nearby buildings. It sounded like the cry of an eagle. And it was audible. Both Bob and Tyler glanced around as they clearly heard it.

"Mom, you can't do this to me!" Addison's voice was coming through me. They were her words crashing out of my vocal cords.

She had somehow taken over my body.

"Get him away from me. Why are you doing this?"

"Addy, baby, your mama is just doing what's best." Tyler's voice was higher pitched than I had expected, but no less oily.

I tried to get Addy to run. We needed to run. Tyler was bad news. I didn't know all the details. I was pretty certain he hit her. I didn't really need to know anything more than she was terrified, and her parents were helping him.

"No, Mom, no." We folded in on ourselves as Addison pulled me down with her.

And with a sudden clarity I didn't know possible, I was in Addison's memories.

27

It felt the way my memories felt. I had all the sensory input from that day. The mesh on the catamaran was bouncy, and I could feel it leaving its imprint on my skin.

I couldn't really smell the ocean, the smell of the life vest was in my nose, or maybe that was whatever they sprayed it down with to disinfect between uses, like bowling shoes. The salt water was an odd combination of cooling mist with sharp pin bricks of stinking bites. Water was odd how it could be both soft and hard.

Mom and Dad were bickering, a lot more than the previous days of the trip. I had hoped that they would have decided they liked each other on this trip. I never understood exactly why they stayed together, let alone how they managed to come up with the idea that I needed this trip after the divorce with Tyler was finalized.

It was all so out of character— the generosity, not the bickering that was normal. I lay back, enjoying the ride, and bouncing on the mesh. At some point, I heard Mom start in on the boat captain about something.

I wanted to ignore it, and wished she would just stop. A

few grumbles from others on this excursion motivated me to move. They wished that lady "would give it a break already." That lady was my mom. If Dad couldn't get her to shut up, maybe I could.

She was gesturing wildly at the captain. And he was doing the same gesturing back. It looked like they were pointing at something. With a twist, I tried to see what they were so concerned about.

Not something, someone.

My heart lodged in my throat as I recognized Tyler standing at the front of an oncoming boat.

Rage filled me. What the hell was going on?

"Mother!" I screamed like a banshee. "What have you done?"

Having no core strength, I sort of flopped and rolled as I pulled myself off of the mesh and onto the decking. I moved like a drunk seal, but much less graceful.

"Addy, you need to calm down." Dad faced me as I crawled off the netting and my feet hit the deck.

I swayed a bit since I didn't have sea legs, and Dad caught me with a bruising grip.

Oh, that explained how I got the fingerprints on my upper arm. I had always assumed that was from someone pulling Addison out of the water.

"Your mother thought having your husband join us would—"

"Ex-husband, Dad. Ex as in not my husband. You know he's not allowed within a hundred yards of my location."

"Well, your mother thought..."

Tears streaked my cheeks. It had taken so much time and effort to get that fucking order of protection against Tyler, and my own mother was blatantly ignoring it.

On wobbly legs, I made my way over to where Mom was still arguing with the captain.

"Mom, whatever you think you're doing, you need to stop. Leave that man alone to do his job."

"Addy," she practically crooned at me. Her demeanor completely the opposite of her treatment of the man driving the big catamaran. "He's being difficult. If he would—"

"Mother, shut up and leave him alone. Captain, I am so sorry for my mother's behavior. If you had a brig, I'd suggest locking her up."

"Addison! How dare you. He needs to pull this thing over immediately so that the little surprise I have for you can take place."

"About that," I grumbled.

Someone in the same t-shirt as the captain came over from a different part of the boat and said something I didn't hear.

"I guess you're getting your way," he said. He shifted something and the boat's engine made a whining sound.

Mom climbed down from the platform where she was crowding the poor man. "That's fabulous, come Addy, I've got someone who wants to see you."

I flinched away from her. "No Mom. Tyler can't be here. He's not supposed to be within a football field of me, and this boat isn't big enough."

"I thought you'd be excited to see him."

"Excited? I left him, got a restraining order, and jumped at the chance to leave the state. Why would I want to see him?"

"He's your husband."

"No, Mom, he is not." Panic began to settle in my chest. I had nowhere to get away from him if he stepped onto this boat.

I wobbled back to the captain. "Can you help me? That man is my ex, I can't be near him."

The captain shrugged. "He's on a Coast Guard boat. Maybe you can tell one of them?"

I crossed to where Mom and Dad stood, waving at the approaching boat.

"Addy, baby!" Tyler yelled and waved.

I ignored him and tried to flag down the attention of anyone else on that boat. It wasn't until they were close enough to throw ropes from one boat to the other that I caught the attention of one of the sailors on the Coast Guard boat.

"He can't be here," I yelled. "I have an order of protection against him, and he cannot come within a hundred yards of me!" I was desperate for someone to listen and help me. Tyler couldn't be here, and yet, all these people were conspiring to put him on the same boat.

That's when the impact happened. At least I think it was an impact. The catamaran rocked and lurched.

People screamed, and I tipped over the edge. With some freakish accident timing, my life vest got caught on something on the catamaran and was pulled easily over my head as I fell into the water without it.

I wasn't the only person in the water, but I was the only one far under the surface and sinking slowly. I smiled and huffed out a wall of bubbles when I realized one of those pairs of legs kicking above me belonged to Tyler. He was wearing those nasty boots he would always track mud into the house with, and then take it out on me when the floors weren't clean.

I floated downward, and twisted, looking at the way the light refracted into the perfect blue depths below me. I could kick my way up, but why? I would have to deal with my parents and Tyler. I would never go back to that man. Never. I wouldn't survive. His violence was on track to be the end of me, sooner than later. I didn't want to be a statistic. And I never wanted to be his victim again.

I turned my attention to the deep. It called to me. I would be safe down there, never to be hurt again.

I made my choice and with a deep breath accepted my fate.

I gasped and sobbed as the memory assaulted my system. I started coughing as if I needed to expell water from my lungs. The memory had been so sharp, so real.

Addison was out of my head, and I was back in Moscow, on my hands and knees on the asphalt of the doctor's office parking lot. I puked all over someone's feet. It wasn't until I felt him grab a fistful of hair that I realized it was Tyler. He hauled me to my feet by my hair. My hands wrapped around his wrists, trying to mitigate the pulling.

"Get off of me," I growled.

I saw Addison as I regained my focus. Her eyes were wide with terror.

I understood now. And I think she finally did too. *Why would mom do that to me?'* she cried.

"And why would you want to stay?" I asked.

"She's been talking crazy," Kristin's voice interrupted my conversation with Addison.

Still in Tyler's grips, I twisted. "This is how you show your daughter love? And you have the nerve to ask why I don't want to be around you?"

Tyler jerked my hair. "Don't talk to your mama that way."

"I said, let me go." This time I didn't acquiesce to the situation. I had spent the last six months swimming and getting stronger. I was stronger than Addison ever had been, mentally and physically. And I wasn't afraid to crack some numb skulls together. The first pair dangled right between Tyler's skinny legs.

I lifted my knee with the determination of a pile driver. I wanted his nuts to explode from the impact, and if not that, I wanted them retreating into his body so far he'd need surgery to find them.

He didn't scream. He sort of did an anti gasp as all the air rushed out of his lungs. He dropped like a lead weight under extra gravity.

"What have you done?" Kristin yelled.

"Boy, are you going to be alright?" Bob asked just as Tyler started to puke.

I didn't care if Tyler was going to be okay or not. I turned out of that parking lot and sprinted. I dashed into the road. Cars honked and swerved as I kept going. I wasn't going to stop until I felt safe, and I wasn't going to feel safe as long as I was in the same state as those people.

I had no way of knowing if Addison stayed or if she was going to follow me. At the moment I was on my own and I kept running. I made it across the street and ran into the grocery store.

"Are you the manager?" I asked the first person I saw who worked there.

They snorted at me. "Do I look like a manager?" I think they took a good look at me at that point and told me to hold tight while they got help.

They came back with a woman in a crisp white shirt and long khaki skirt. "Come with me, we'll get you some help."

She led me into a back room, and helped me into a chair. The kid I talked to first came back with a paper cup full of cold water.

"Thank you," I managed after a few minutes of catching

my breath. "Can I stay back here until my ride shows up?" I waggled my phone at her.

"Are you sure? Are you safe? You look pretty shaken up, terrified actually," she said.

I nodded as I typed into the app where I was and where I wanted to go. "I am now, I think. My ex just tried to get me into his truck. I nailed him pretty hard with my knee. I just need to get out of town, and I'll be fine," I explained.

"And you have a way out? You don't need help getting to a shelter, do you?"

"Can I hug you?" I asked.

She looked very nervous as she held out her arms and accepted my hug. I took her hands in mine and made eye contact. I think she had been on the verge of tears.

"You are the first person to ask if I was safe. My own mother was trying to get me to go back. I have a way and the means to get out of town. But I want to thank you for being willing to help when you didn't know if I did or not."

"Someone helped me once," she admitted.

"I thought so."

My phone app pinged that my ride was out front.

"Thank you." I squeezed her hand again.

She pulled me in for a second hug, and then I was out of the store and climbing into the car waiting for me.

"Are you serious, you'll pay for me to take you all the way to the airport in Spokane and back?" My driver said as I settled into the back.

"Yeah, if that's okay with you," I answered.

"Easiest money I've made in a while. You don't mind if I play some tunes, do you?"

"No, but we do need to stop at my hotel to grab my bags first."

28

Adrenaline coursed through my veins. The driver's tunes, a playlist of louder rap and hip-hop, kept my energy up the entire drive. It helped the time to go by much faster.

Addy sat in the far corner from me, her eyes wide. She trembled with what I could only imagine as the fear of realizing what she thought her family was like versus the reality she had just come face to face with.

I felt like howling with triumph every time I recalled the satisfying impact of my thigh against Tyler's groin. I hit him hard. Really hard, as evidenced with his collapse and throwing up. It was a win I could not crow about in the moment. I had been as scared as Addy. And it was on me to get the both of us out of there as fast as I could.

Now we were safe, surrounded by music that felt powerful and appropriate. It felt like warrior's music to my nerves.

Not quite an hour into the ride, I realized I needed to acknowledge the angel that helped us. I hadn't gotten her name, but if she was the store manager, I should be able to find her easily enough. My cell connection was spotty, but I was used to working with crap connectivity on the ship. I wrote my letter to corporate letting them know of this angel who went above and beyond for her community.

When I had a second of connection, I was able to find her name and drop it into my letter. The next spot of connection, I located the leave a comment link. I was able to cut and paste my letter into the appropriate window.

The next time I had bars, the letter would automatically send. I also looked up the email for corporate HQ, and did the same. She may have only given us refuge and some water, but she saved me. She saved Addy, and Addy saw that there were people willing to protect her, not put her in harms way, the way her mother so blatantly had.

The store manager had been the angel in the moment Addy needed her. All of my railing against the life Addy had been trapped in was nothing compared to those simple moments of grace that woman had shown us. I wasn't anybody's angel, I was well aware of that.

I glanced at the space where Addy had been. She was gone. Maybe she faded when she went to sleep. Maybe she had run away to wherever it was she went.

When I had been like Addy, without a body, I was aware of locations and of people. And between times, I wasn't aware of anything. I couldn't say now where I had gone in times like these. Had I forgotten in my time in this body? Or was it something I had never been aware of?

As airports are, it was a hive of frenetic energy. I gave my driver a hefty cash tip, in addition to the sizable tip I left in the app. I was grateful on many levels for him being available to drive me all this way, and into another state.

"You have a good trip!" he said as he left me and my bags along the check in curb.

I didn't feel like I could relax or let my guard down until the plane touched down in Florida.

Traveling with layovers and connections were not soothing. Once I had medical clearance from the doctor in Moscow, I needed to get a drivers license. I didn't claim residency in Idaho, and I never would. Especially after that terrifying greeting from Addison's family. I never wanted to set foot in Idaho again.

Technically, I didn't have residency anywhere the government recognized. I lived on a boat. So I shared a legal residency with Dirk and Patty, and half of the crew of *Cherry Ala Mode* in Tampa at PIE's Florida offices. I had only ever been here to visit the office, and funny enough, never by ship.

Cherry Ala Mode tended to stay in the South Pacific, or along the west coast of the Americas. It wasn't PIE's only ship. Strandfield bounced around between the ships quite a bit. He wasn't merely a boat's captain, he was the head of all the oceanic vessels for the organization.

I lugged everything I had into my motel room for the night. I was here long enough to pick up notarized documents from the office, and have Lauren, the office manager, take me to get a driver's test.

I stared at my boxes. What was I going to do with them?

I had pictured my jaunt across the continent a little less encumbered than it turned out to be. I had boxes of notes that I needed to decide if I was going to keep, or if their digital counterparts were enough. I didn't want to pay for indefinite storage. Maybe I would dump them on Collin. After all, my notes were taken on his field site. And it all supported his and Dr. Nakamura's research. Maybe he'd be interested in having them?

But that meant having to haul them back across the

continent and halfway across the Pacific. I tore open the box on the top of the stack and pulled out the notebook on top.

It was full of my chicken scratch notes. And every scribble brought back a memory. Before I knew it, I was sitting in the middle of the bed surrounded by stacks of notebooks. This notebook reminded me of how Bro was constantly stretching or twitching out dance steps with little movements that in his head had to encompass the full range of motion. That notebook was written on the day he said he would help me, but I ended up having to do all the lifting and carrying because he tweaked his shoulder.

Every memory was a slap in the face of how he wasn't really there. And I hadn't noticed at all.

The next morning, Lauren arrived at my motel room bright and early.

"What's all that?" She pointed to my boxes.

"Notes. I had them in storage in Hawaii, but now I don't know what to do with them. You have everything I need?"

I closed the door behind me and followed her to the car.

"Not so fast," she said. "Let's load everything up, you can check out of the hotel now and not have to double back."

"I didn't think you'd want all that stuff in your car," I explained.

"Why don't you put those boxes in your storage locker, and then you only have to worry about your suitcase."

"Well, that's just it. I pulled them out of storage because I didn't want to keep paying for them to sit on an island I didn't know if I'd ever get back to. Storing them in Florida seems even more out of the way."

"Did you forget you have a locker at the office for things just like this?" Lauren asked. Her hand was still on the door to my room, expecting me to open it back up.

Apparently, I had.

"Not only does this place provide you with a permanent address for residency, you can keep your stuff here for when you're on the ship. Most of you live on the ship and don't keep a place state side."

"I hadn't realized," I confessed. Then again, I hadn't had any other belongings to worry about before this.

With Lauren's guidance, I stored my few boxes in my new-to-me storage locker at the P.I.E. offices. She went over all the necessary documents I would need, including the notary stamped document for proof of residence. And then she handed me a small newsprint booklet.

"What's this for?" I asked as I accepted it.

"That's for your driver's test. I hope you're a quick study."

I let out a low grumble. Hopefully driving rules hadn't changed too much from the last time I took the written test. Then again, that had been a different century. The entire world had changed. I crammed as she took the long way to the Department of Motor Vehicles.

Nerves twisted in my stomach once I was back in Hawaii. I was safe from the Rouche-Jones situation, but now I wondered if I would see Bro again any time soon. Or had I completely lost him after that argument in Fiji?

The physical aspect of Addison's life was now completely left behind. This body was now Mancey Amador, I had all the IDs to prove it, and it was medically cleared of all of Addison's medical baggage. The next time she manifested, we were going to have to come to an understanding. Of course, I had no idea if she was even going to come back.

I hoped she was happy wherever she ended up. That confrontation with the parents and Tyler had to have been ground shattering traumatic. It had shaken me up, and I hadn't trusted those people to begin with. Addy had loved them.

The little bungalow I rented for a few weeks was perfect. A short walk to the beach, and not so far away that I couldn't get a ride to Emi, or she could come visit me.

The plan was to hang out, have a real vacation. It was time to give myself a break without strategizing how I would win Collin Paulo's affection. I knew that was no longer a possibility. I hoped he got his head out of his ass long enough to really see Leia. She was perfect for him.

It was time for me to appreciate the beach and just being here.

I was still too pale to take on the beach without adequate protection. Sunscreen and a parasol were my friends. People in Asia understood the logic of a good parasol. And European women back in the day did too. I would never understand why they went out of fashion. I had shade and protection, and a stylish accessory.

29

———

The car stopped in the driveway. I thanked the driver as I climbed out from the back. It was disconcerting to approach the house from this direction. I had spent several months just popping in and out at free will.

Then again my "life" as it were, had been so completely different. Before I could approach the front stoop, a little boy with messy brown hair stopped from a dead run near the giant fern at the corner of the house. "We're in the back!" He yelled before darting off again.

With a slight shrug, I changed course and walked around the side of the house. The magical landscape that had been Emi's wedding had converted back to a beloved backyard. But I did notice the party lights were still strung around the edges of the patio, and now better furniture populated the place.

And just as I had been expecting, Emi was relaxing in a lounge chair with her feet up.

"Macey!" she exclaimed as I came into view. "I was beginning to wonder when we'd ever see you again." She held her hand out to me, as if she were the lingering starlet.

I crossed the yard before she levered herself out of the chair. Her baby bump was less bump and more like Moana Kea.

"Look at you! You're glowing," I declared.

"Uh, it's sweat. I'm sweating all the time. So sweaty, it's gross," she complained.

I tilted my head to where Hamilton was playing. "You're not the only one who is getting bigger. Is he taller?"

"He's like freaking kudzu. Blink and he's taller, his feet are bigger, nothing fits. Do you want something to drink? I have some lemonade in the kitchen."

I volunteered to get us a couple of glasses. I did remember where everything was, even though I hadn't been inside this house in this lifetime.

"Our changes are obvious, I mean you can just look at us and tell what's been going on. What the hell happened to you?" Emi asked as I handed over a tall glass.

I parked my butt in an available chair and let my body relax. This yard felt as close to home as any place had in a very long time. I needed to get a yard I could relax in.

"I've been finding myself. I was struggling with who I was for so long. It was more than just a name thing. I had to deal with the ghost of Addison and her family."

"Literally or figuratively?" Emi asked.

"A bit of both. I was struggling with being someone I wasn't, and expected to have their memories. It was hard, especially when Addy wasn't sharing."

Emi's brows raised.

I nodded. "Yeah, she was hanging out, when it was convenient for her. But not for me. She couldn't decide what she wanted, and if a situation got tough, she'd ghost on me." I laughed at my own joke. "I thought she was gone for good, but it wasn't until I got off the boat that she came back. And

I found out why. She fell off a boat, so yeah, me living on a boat for almost six months had her long gone."

"So, how was it?" Emi asked. "I can't believe you walked straight into a research position with some oceanic group."

"Me either. When Strandfield first approached me, I thought he was going to chew me out for running off with his boat and two of his scientists. But no, he showed up at my hotel room and invited me to come play with them immediately. It's been great."

"Are you going back?" A deep voice asked.

I turned to see who it was at the same time Emi said, "Collin, what are you doing here?"

Collin strode into Emi's side of the yard from their parent's home. He was as handsome as ever, but his hair seemed a bit shorter, more stylish. He wore what I had come to consider his uniform, cargo shorts. Bright blue K-tape stripes lined the back of his calf. I had only thought Bro had used the therapeutic tape, having never actually seen it on Collin before. Instead of his standard collard polo, he wore a character t-shirt, stretched tight across his chest, and straining at his massive biceps.

It wasn't his impressive physique that took my breath. Slightly behind him hovered Bro. Only he didn't appear as solid as the last time I had seen him. This time I could tell he was non-corporeal. I didn't know how to deal with his presence. Ignoring him might not have been the smart thing to do, but it's the option I took.

"You're wearing a Pele and Pete t-shirt." I said, pronouncing Pele as peh-ley. I doubted I would ever forgive myself for having mispronounced so badly it outloud in front of other people. I probably still butchered proper pronunciation, but at least I wasn't saying *peel*.

He gave a little shrug. "Yeah, well, I came to realize that it's actually not as embarrassing as I had been thinking."

"It's never been embarrassing, you're just an idiot," Emi said. "Go grab yourself a drink."

She pointed him into the house. Bro followed him inside.

I leaned closer to Emi. "Do you see someone or something behind your brother?"

"Like what?"

I bugged my eyes out at her and grimaced.

"Oh, you mean like a ghost?" She lowered her voice into a whisper. "No ghosts. But he sparkles a little, and he's got a few orbs floating around him."

I nodded. "That must be what I'm picking up."

"You don't see the orbs, do you?"

I shook my head. "Not anymore. I thought there was a shimmer."

So Emi didn't see Bro. I was going to have to deal with him at some point. Only, I didn't know how.

Collin stepped out of the back door. I expected it to slam shut, but it didn't.

"You got the door fixed," I said to Emi before turning my attention back to Collin and his shirt. "Did Leia set you straight about that?"

Collin rubbed his hand up the back of his neck and over the short hair on the back of his head, and looked down. Was he blushing? He sat and took a long drink without saying anything.

"It was Leia!" I exclaimed.

"Who is Leia?" Emi asked.

"She's ah..." Collin started.

'Are you just going to pretend I'm not here?' Bro asked.

I held up my hand at Bro. *'I'll talk to you later.'* I don't think he heard me the way Addy could with my in-head talk to the ghost method, because he kept glaring at me.

It looked like I was shutting Collin up.

"She's gorgeous," I gushed. "One of his graduate students. And before you say anything about her being young, she's an older grad student. Had to take a couple of years off after getting her bachelor's before grad school. And she should be graduating soon."

"What does that have to do with anything?" Emi asked.

I kept talking, not that I expected Collin to be forthcoming with answers, but I think he needed to hear this too. "Once she graduates, there's no professor student fraternization problems. And Emi, she is a beautiful dancer. And so smart. She'll be at the competition tomorrow, won't she?"

"I didn't think you two got along." Collin said with a nod.

"We didn't, don't. She never trusted me, rightly so. But Collin, she is perfect for you. Trust me when I say this. You have to talk to her."

He shook his head. "She hasn't graduated yet."

"Wait, Collin has a girlfriend?" Emi giggled.

"I don't have a girlfriend," he grumbled. "I didn't come here to get berated over a t-shirt."

"It's about way more than the t-shirt," I said.

"Says you," he countered. "Are you an expert in dating advice now? Addison Rouche? Or is that Manchester? Who are you even? You showed up at my fieldwork lab brandishing a forged letter of introduction. Idaho State University has never heard of you, in any of your aliases, and they do not have a tectonics research division."

"You looked me up?" My nerves clenched for a brief moment of panic.

Collin glowered in my direction. The man had expressed more emotion in this short interaction than he had the entire time I had worked alongside his team out at the lava flow.

"I looked you up." He set his glass down and crossed his arms with an air of finality.

Letting out a long sigh, I relaxed back into the chair. The truth was out, no more having to pretend. "I faked it. All of it."

"Including the data you collected? Your research?"

"That's the only thing that turned out to be real about the whole situation. The GeoTalker actually worked. I have so much data to support the thesis. It's why I stayed with PIE for so long."

"Pie? You make no sense, woman."

"P.I.E. Poseidon Institute of Exploration. I've been living and working on a ship for almost six months for a reason. The GeoTalker worked, and they helped me expand my research to gather data from underwater volcanoes. The paper is about to be published. You and Dr. Nakamura are well cited and credited. I'll make sure you get a copy without having to pay any of those scientific journal fees. Also, you can have access to any of the data you might need or want, at any time."

He stared at me blinking for a long moment. His face locked in an expression of consternation. He wanted to be angry with me, but I essentially just handed him a ton of relevant resource data for his work on a silver platter.

"That doesn't explain who you are, just your work," Collin grumbled in a very familiar way.

'He's right. Who are you really?' Bro grumbled. I could tell he did not like the way I was ignoring him.

"Let's just say I'm a wealthy, eccentric private researcher who felt the need for some subterfuge in order to be taken seriously, initially." I tipped my drink at him before taking a sip. It was almost perfect, a little on the tart side.

"Wealthy?" Emi asked.

"Insurance payout. Boating companies don't like it when you fall overboard and die. Neither does the Coast Guard when it turns out their boat contributed to the accident."

Collin's face looked stricken.

Emi's brows went up, but she nodded. She had been there shortly after the accident that landed me in this body.

"Don't freak out," I said. "It happened a while ago."

"Almost a year?" Emi asked.

I thought about it for a moment. I didn't have the date engraved in my memory. Maybe if Addison had decided to stick around, she would have remembered. Her mother certainly would have. "Yeah, probably a little longer than that. I don't exactly recall."

"So, you decided to do whatever you wanted to do?" he asked.

I shrugged. "The point is, Collin, I realized life is too short to waste it following other people's dimwitted rules, especially when they don't benefit you. Go find Leia at the next competition, ask her out for dinner. And if you are going to stick rigidly to those non-fraternization boundaries, tell her. Tell her you want to take her out as soon as she graduates because you won't be her professor any longer, and you like her. I'd be surprised if she said no. She's probably waiting for graduation so she can ask you out." I turned my attention from Collin to Emi. "Seriously, she is feisty and won't put up with this guy's nonsense. She knew I was full of bullshit from the get-go. They actually know each other from dance competitions, which I think proves it wouldn't be inappropriate if they started dating now."

"She sounds kind of perfect," Emi said.

"She kind of is," Collin admitted.

I never expected to feel so happy to hear Collin admit he was attracted to someone else. Then again, I had been ecstatic for Emi when she and Jeremy finally figured things out. My friends deserved to be happy. And while I knew Collin wasn't a friend, he wasn't exactly not one either.

30

After a long afternoon on the beach, I made my way back to my little rental bungalow. I waffled wildly between reveling in being on my own, enjoying my own company, and hating the silence that surrounded me.

I was never all alone on the ship. Someone was always around if I needed company. And I could sequester myself away when I wanted to be left alone. But this was different. I really only knew Emi, and I wasn't about to barge in on her growing family at two in the morning because I got bored and lonely.

It was different because I expected Addy to show up at any moment and begin interrogating me over what happened back in that parking lot before I ran, we ran. It had been days since I had seen her. At least now I understood why I hadn't had the pleasure of her company on board the Cherry. But this was the beach.

Same for Bro. Why hadn't he tried to come find me? Did he still think he was among the living?

I stripped down on the back porch, before coating my skin with baby powder. I brushed the powder and as much sand as possible off, leaving it all behind. This place was quaint and lovely. Too bad there wasn't an outdoor shower, or the bathroom wasn't closer to the back door.

Island living, especially being on the beach daily, meant sand in the house. I could handle sand in uncomfortable places when I was where the sand dominated, meaning the beach. But I couldn't stand it in my living space. More than once I had to get out of bed, shower and change my sheets because I had not been meticulous enough about cleaning up anything I may have tracked into the house.

I didn't feel like following my self-imposed routine about sweeping after I stepped from the shower. Remembering how unfun it was to change the sheets in the middle of the night had me sweeping the floor before I got dressed.

I would never be able to live like this full time. I was too wrapped up in my little luxuries to properly live on the beach. Even though it was beautiful.

I finished sweeping, rinsed my feet off again, and got dressed to be in for the rest of the evening. Dinner was ice cream straight from the carton. I was an adult, and I could have ice cream if I wanted. There was never enough ice cream on the ship.

There was nothing interesting on television. I checked and spent hours scrolling through the channels looking for something to keep me entertained. The knock on the door was practically a relief. If nothing else, it was a proper distraction.

I glanced out the window before opening the door. I wasn't expecting anybody, and I certainly didn't expect Bro to knock. He could come and go as he liked. It was obvious that he didn't realize he was a ghost.

"What are you doing here?" I asked as I opened the door.

"Do you have any idea how hard it was for me to find you?"

I shrugged. But I stepped back, giving him room to step inside. "Probably not as hard as you made it."

"It's like that, huh?" he snapped. "Why did you ignore me the other day?"

"Why did you walk out on me in Fiji?" I snapped right back.

"You admitted you had done everything for Collin. How was I supposed to take that?"

I rolled my eyes. I tossed up my hands as I stepped back into the small living room. I picked up a couch pillow and hugged it to my front as if it were some type of shield. I spun, folded my leg, and sat with it tucked up under me.

Bro decided to stand and pace. He grunted like an angry bull. He sort of looked like one, all hunched up heavy shoulder muscles and wild hair. Damn, I had missed him. But him being here now didn't change the fact that he was dead. He was a ghost. Only he didn't know it.

"Brody Nakamura, who was in my bed? You or Collin?"

He stopped his back and forth and stared at me. "What was I, some consolation prize?"

I laughed.

"You flirted with me at the wedding, and then you go and tell me you set everything up for Collin. How am I supposed to feel?" He swiped his hand through the air as if pushing something away from him before restarting his pacing.

"I flirted with quite a few men at that wedding. Including George O'Connell. I don't see you losing your shit over that. And George O'Connell is a movie star," I pointed out.

Bro glowered and grumbled. "That's not the same."

"It very much is the same. I exchanged witty banter with a man who clearly found me attractive, and I did not end up in bed with him. How is that different? Oh right, I did eventually end up in bed with you. You Bro, not George, not Collin, not anyone else. So what if Collin was my motivation?"

Bro stopped walking again, this time his shoulders and posture slumped. He looked deflated. "But Collin."

I let the silence hang in the air between us.

"But Collin nothing. Look, I don't know if you're mad that you think I made you break some kind of code where you don't filch your friend's lovers, or if you're mad I met Collin long before I met you. Or what, but you need to understand I'm also mad at you."

His ire was back up, the angry bull reinflated. "What did I do?"

I shook my head. The laundry list of his transgressions was a long one. I let out a heavy sigh and patted the couch next to me. "You're gonna want to sit down first."

I turned toward him as he sat. "Look, Bro. I want to apologize for how I tried to confess about how I came into your life. I wanted you to know that while I did do it for Collin initially, my motivations changed."

"Leia?"

I shook my head. Leia had very little to do with it. "I didn't know him. I thought my insane instant attraction to him was enough. It never occurred to me that he wouldn't blink twice in my direction or give me the time of day."

Bro shifted and cleared his throat. "Vain much?"

I let out a bitter laugh. "You have no idea. It didn't take me very long to realize I was barking up the wrong tree. And while I was coming to the conclusion, he was not for me, two other very important things happened."

Bro's eyebrow lifted.

"The science started working. And you. I didn't expect you." I reached out my hand toward him.

He took it and carefully threaded his fingers between mine. It felt like electric static. It felt like forgiveness. It felt like he had missed me too.

"You said you met Collin first. I can't rectify the five minute difference in my head. Or here." He pressed our intertwined hands to his heart.

He felt so warm and solid. It made no sense.

"Five minutes?" I asked.

"Yeah, at the wedding."

I shook my head. "I first met Collin long before the wedding. And to show you just how insignificant I am to him, he is clueless about that."

"And if you had met me first, would you have done all of that to get my attention?"

I shook my head. "I wouldn't have needed to. You saw me right away. But just so you know, it was for you that I kept working on the research. I wanted to prove your theories were correct."

"My theories?"

I put the pillow down and scooted in closer. "Dr. Brody Nakamura, it was your theory about communication signals from active volcanos that was really behind all of my work."

"Collin..." he started.

"Collin picked up your theory and began the work with you. He continues the work. You've influenced his entire life, and mine."

His brow furrowed. The grip he had on my hand lessened.

"This sounds like some of that crap you were babbling about past lives. What's going on, Mancey?"

I held on tight even while he was letting go. "It wasn't crap, Bro. When were you born?"

Confusion creased his brow further. "October fifteenth, why?"

I shook my head. "What year?"

His head tilted to the side.

"How old are you?"

He looked down and patted his chest with his free hand.

"Do you know how old you are, Bro?"

With panic in his eyes, he locked eyes with me and shook his head. "Mancey, what's going on? Why can't I remember?"

"Do you remember why you couldn't go to Tonga with me?"

He looked away. "I was angry. I couldn't keep doing it."

"Doing what?" I prodded gently. I wanted, no needed, him to realize he couldn't go to Tonga because the reason he was going had actually killed him.

He ran his hand through his hair. "I couldn't get on that damned boat again."

I released the breath I had been holding. He found it.

"This is going to be a lot to take in." I stood and crossed the room to the dining table. I picked up the laptop I now used for my work, and for keeping in touch with the few people I emailed regularly, Emi and Sadie.

I navigated to the folder I kept on Bro. My excuse for keeping it was for the research, but honestly, it was to maintain a connection to him. The man died long before I ever met him.

"Look at this," I said as I sat down next to him. I placed the computer in front of him and swiveled it so he could see the first article I had opened.

It featured a picture of him and Collin. Collin was in his late twenties, Bro, his late sixties.

"Photoshop," he declared. "That's me, I remember that day, but we're the same age."

I shook my head.

"We grew up together," Bro stated.

"No, Bro. You watched Collin and his brother and sister grow up. You were friends with his parents." I pulled up a different picture. Him with Collin's dad.

"You're the family friend who created Pele and Pete. You were the influence behind Collin studying local geology, and dancing."

He pushed to his feet. "I don't believe you. I'm not some seventy-year-old man. Look at me. I'm... I'm..." he faltered. "I'm in my prime."

"You're not an old man Bro because—" I swallowed. This was hard, much harder than I realized it would be "—you're dead. You're a ghost."

I didn't expect his sharp bark of derision. "Not that bullshit again. Are you a ghost too?"

His eyes went wide, and he wiggled his fingers while making a spooky O shape with his mouth.

"Not anymore," I admitted with a shake of my head.

He leaned forward and closed my laptop. He continued to lean in closer to me. I should have been able to feel his breath against my face, but there was no breath. It was the first time I could tell he wasn't actually alive.

"If I'm a ghost, how can I do this?" He reached out and lifted a lock of my hair.

"I don't know," I admitted. My breath caught. He was so close, and I missed him so much.

"Or this?" His lips against mine were gentle.

I expected him to punish me somehow, to take out on

me his frustration and confusion. But he didn't bruise me with his lips. He continued leaning into my space until I was on my back against the cushions, and he held himself above me.

"Do I feel like some old man?" He brushed his chest against mine.

My nipples peaked at the sensation.

"If I were a ghost, how would I be able to feel you?" He ran his hand over my ribs before cupping a breast.

I wiggled into his grip. I didn't know how it worked. At the moment, I didn't care. I had Bro back, and he was touching me.

I ran my leg up his. His skin was warm and smooth against mine. He felt very much solid and present. I skimmed my hands under his t-shirt. And that's when I recognized the sensation of electrical buzzing in my fingertips, the clue that I wasn't touching a living, breathing man. I was touching his very being, his energy.

I felt his need of me as he pressed his hips to mine. Whatever there was between us, that intense need was still there.

I tugged at his shirt. He sat back on his knees to pull it off. I watched him with a heated gaze as he exposed his chest. He was my Bro. I felt a pang of guilt or remorse in my gut momentarily. I knew this couldn't last between us. He wasn't really here.

He tugged at my clothes, and I stopped worrying about the logistics of making love to a spirit. He didn't seem bothered by the enterprise. The only thing that bothered him at the moment were our clothes. And we discarded them as quickly as possible

His mouth was hot and warm against mine, and that's all that mattered. He kissed across my chest and down my middle. His fingers gripped my hips with a bruising force. I now understood why I never bruised no matter how intensely he manhandled me.

I spread my thighs for his kiss. I screamed and moaned as he did magical things to me with his tongue. I fisted his hair in my hands as he masterfully took me to the brink of orgasm before he stopped.

I whimpered. "No, don't stop."

He stood and lifted me into his arms. "I much prefer a bed. Which way."

I languidly pointed behind me toward the bedroom.

He gently placed me in the center of the bed, and then proceeded to make me completely boneless. He filled me completely, and battered into me so delectably. I was reduced to mewing and moaning against his masterful touch and multiple orgasms.

He roared out his own release, and I laughed as I saw how completely undone he became. I loved how we made each other overwhelmed with desire, and how we drained each other completely.

In the morning, I woke, draped across his massive chest.

"You awake?" he asked.

I rolled off him with a groan. I was, but I had been happier asleep using him as a mattress.

"I missed you," I confessed as I leaned back to claim a kiss. I knew this would be one of the last ones I would ever have from him.

"I missed you too." He sat up. "So, is that how a ghost feels?"

"I guess so," I said. My gut tightened as I recognized our romantic interlude was over.

"You know I don't believe any of that crap you said?"

"I do."

"You still think I'm some kind of ghost?"

I pulled the sheet around me as I followed his naked ass out to the living room to find his clothes. He was a beautiful sight, even as he covered his gorgeous body with his stupid cargo shorts and old surfing t-shirt. And always, the same beat up pair of flip-flops.

"Brody Nakamura, I love you," I said.

He looked at me and shook his head. "You know, I thought I was in love with you once. But Mancey, I'm not gonna put up with your crazy."

"I know you aren't. And I'm not crazy. Why couldn't you come to Tonga with me?"

"I told you, I couldn't. That charter boat captain almost got us all killed. I wasn't going to put myself back into a situation like that."

He seemed to be remembering more.

"You're getting closer to the truth," I muttered.

"If you think you know, why play these games with me?" He stood cross armed and angry in the middle of the living room. He looked much like he had the night before, only his hair was more wild from our night's activities.

"You couldn't go to Tonga with me because that's where you died."

He let out a sharp bark of a laugh. "I died in Tonga? Right." He spun on his heel and pushed out through the front door.

I followed with quick scurrying steps.

"That island we were going to, Hunga Tonga–Hunga Ha'apai, collapsed in a volcanic eruption. Your boat got caught too close to the island. Bro, you died, and I had to have some stranger tell me about it." I tried to yell out after him, but he was already gone.

I folded in on myself and collapsed to the floor. I loved

him, and I could have kept him if I had only kept the truth to myself. But I couldn't do that. I hadn't found a way back to the living only to fall in love with a ghost. After everything I had been through, what Addy had been through, I deserved a living lover. I still cried and was dramatic and moody about it.

31

───────

The sand was cooler the deeper I dug my toes in.

It was late enough in the evening that I had my parasol collapsed and laying at my side. The sun was low somewhere to the west, casting long shadows.

I stared out at the waves and the flat looking ocean beyond. I knew those cool blue waves were deceptive, it was all rolling hills and mountains out there. I was deep in my emotions this evening. Is this what people referred to as shadow work? I had to come to terms with my mortality and existence?

It all stemmed from the ocean. Everything, my life, hell, life in general. But the connection I now felt seemed more intense. It was the ocean where Addy found her strength, and through that event I regained life. It was all so metaphysical and profound.

I felt alone for the first time in a very long time. I wiped a tear away. This was the kind of moment it would have been nice to have a strong broad shoulder to lean against. I was being maudlin in my solitude.

"What are you doing out here?"

A familiar voice caught me off guard and I flinched.

"Man, you're jumpy," Addy said as she sat next to me. "What's this for?"

I moved the folded up umbrella to my other side. "Sun shade."

She lifted her head up to the sky. "There's no sun right now."

I gave her a soft smile that hid the exasperation I felt. There was no sun now, but there had been hours earlier when I had come out to the beach. "That's why it's folded up now."

"You know the sunset is on the other side of the island, right?"

"Yes, I know that. It's why all those expensive hotels and resorts are on those beaches. That's also where all the people are." And was why the rent on my bungalow was ever so slightly less. Not that there weren't plenty of people on the beach with me now, but the mass of tourists had left long before the dinner hour.

"I can still see the sky change and the tide get restless," I said, feeling wistful.

"Is this what we're doing now?" Addy asked.

"It's what I'm doing. You can do whatever you want."

"I don't know what I want," she admitted.

I rubbed at the center of my chest. The memory of her accident should have made my lungs burn. But that's not what she had been feeling at the time.

"You're probably not going to like to hear this, but when you were drowning—"

"I felt free. Yeah, I totally remember that." She cut me off.

I wiggled my toes more, loving the sense of being integrated into the ground, as if I were being planted.

"Really? Because you've been acting like you want to go right back into the arms of the problem."

"You mean Tyler and my parents, don't you?"

I nodded.

"I think I wanted to forget about all of that. I wanted both, I wanted the freedom you seemed to have as me, but I also wanted to be me. That meant having those ties to my parents and home." She held up her hand to stop me from saying anything. "I was wrong. If that had been me, I wouldn't have run. I would have let them take me, and I would have been scared and miserable. But not you. Oh my God, the way you cracked Tyler's balls! I never would have been able to do that. I think that's why drowning seemed like the best choice. He'd have killed me eventually if I stayed. I guess he did kill me, didn't he? He's why I fell in the water to begin with."

She sat in silence with her thoughts for a long moment.

"But you had wanted to go back," I eventually pointed out.

"I had completely forgotten. That's not the kind of memory you want to hold on to. You were trying to protect us, and I kept trying to drag us back into the lion's den."

"Now what?" I asked. "You just gonna hang out with me now? That's going to be hard, I'm getting back on that ship next month."

Addy stared out over the water the same way I was, as if the answers were out there.

"What are my options? I don't want to be a ghost watching someone else live in my body. That's just creepy and weird. I mean, you were once in my position, right?"

I nodded. "Other than having someone else in my body. Yeah, I was hanging out watching people have their lives."

"What did you do?" she asked.

"I drifted around for the longest time before I found Emi. And she could see and talk to me. It wasn't until then that I went and got a life for myself. I don't know how it happened, I just knew it was time for me to have a body, and the next thing I clearly remember is regaining consciousness in this body."

"So, I can just decide I want to jump into someone's body? After seeing all the trouble I've caused you, I don't think I want to do that."

"So stay a ghost. Speaking of being a ghost, why didn't you tell me about Bro?"

"Who?" She genuinely sounded confused.

"Brody, the guy I was seeing." I couldn't quite vocalize that I had been sleeping with a ghost. Still wasn't sure how any of that had happened.

"You dated someone on the boat? Duh, boat, I wasn't there," she said, her old attitude slipped back in.

"Not on the boat, before the boat. At the volcano. Bro, the dancer."

"You mean Collin?"

I rolled my eyes. "No, the other guy, the one who I found out had died a couple of years ago. The ghost." I shrugged.

Her jaw went slack and she shook her head. "I never saw another ghost. Are there any? I'm the only one around."

"Huh?" When I had been non-corporeal, I was aware of other spirits. Maybe Addy really hadn't been aware of Bro. He certainly never indicated he was aware of her. Then again, he hadn't been aware he was dead either. I sat in silence for a long moment, trying to mix everything up together and come up with an answer, like ingredients for a cake, or cookies.

"I bet you could reincarnate," I finally blurted out.

"Start from scratch? What if the family I end up with is even worse?"

"Then you're stuck being a ghost unless you want to move on," I said.

"Move on? You mean heaven?"

"I guess. I don't know if I necessarily believe in the whole heaven and hell thing, especially after being non-corporeal as long as I was. But yeah. There is a beyond from where you are now. No ties to this earth, or the people here. I would like to think it's a heaven of sorts."

Addy sighed. "A heaven of sorts sounds nice. Not having to worry about anything, not having to question if today is the day he snaps because I made spaghetti, and he wanted a cheeseburger."

"You could be free of earthly bonds. Remember the freedom and peace you got from the ocean?"

Addy stood. She was shimmering. It was the first time I had ever seen her look like that.

She turned to smile down at me. I think it was the first time I had ever seen a smile on her face. It changed everything about her, and made me think she had definitely not smiled enough in her life. She was beautiful, and the joy that emanated from her vibrated with euphoria.

"I can be free." It wasn't a question, but a statement. She realized she had control. "Thank you, Mancey. I hope you and our body have a wonderful life. I guess it's your body now. Thank you."

She started moving toward the water. As she slowly walked, the very nature of her being changed. It was as if she filled with sparkles and light. The Addy-ness of the shape faded, and glittering light swirled like shooting stars in an ever expanding ball of energy. What had been Addison became one with the air and the sky.

I was overcome with peace and a lifting of burdens, like a cool wash running over my skin. Addy found her peace. I hoped her heaven was what she needed. She deserved a better after life than the life she had endured. And that included the bullshit she had to put up with from me.

I continued to sit and wiggle my toes in the sand until long after the sun set. Addy had found a way to move on with her existence. It was time for me to do the same. I wiped sand from my backside and legs and gathered my beach gear and headed back to my bungalow. My days of sitting on the beach were coming to an end. I needed to figure out how to find Bro, or get him to find me again.

I'd be attending a dance festival with Emi in a couple of days. Hamilton was going to have his first big performance. There was no way I was going to miss that. Even though he no longer remembered who he had been, I still liked that kid immensely and wanted to cheer him on. I really hoped Bro would be there. We needed to talk some more.

32

I met Emi at the entrance of the convention center. I had expected her to be waddling, but her baby bump wasn't nearly as prominent as she had been making it when I visited her. Her father carried her bags for her. I knew those bags were full of snacks, having come to one of these shows with her before.

We would be ensconced in the riser seats for hours. But it was worth it. Today's competition was extra special. Hamilton practically vibrated at her side, he had a duffle bag almost as large as himself over his shoulder. It was his first performance in front of a big audience.

"You'll be terrific," I said to him.

His eyes were wide, the only hint of nerves in his excited state. I had given up teasing him about how we had been friends in a different life. I realized it was creepy. And that was not the kind of person I wanted to be.

"I'll go get Hami checked in, and I'll come find you. Don't get seats too far up," Emi directed.

"We've got it," her dad said. "You'll do just fine. If you get overwhelmed, remember everyone out here is cheering you on, no matter what. Focus on all that positive energy coming at you."

"I'm here, let's go," Jeremy announced as he jogged up to our little group. He must have been parking the car.

Once inside, we split. Jeremy and Emi took Hami backstage, and her father and I headed for the stands.

"You gave advice like you've been in front of a big crowd." I was nervous for Hami. I had never performed in front of a big audience. All of my work had been done in front of camera crews. But I was a pro when it came to waving and looking pretty in front of adoring fans. "Emi never mentioned it, but were you a performer? Did you dance like Collin?"

I really wanted to ask him how he had known Bro. But that would have been intrusive and weird. I was a random friend of his daughter's who he had barely met at her wedding. It would have felt stalkery and invasive to suddenly ask about his personal life when no one had brought it up. I didn't want to be like that. If Bro showed up today, and I had the chance, I'd ask him.

Emi's father carried half the genes that made his children so good looking. His prime was well past him. Not that he wasn't still a good looking man, but I didn't ogle my friend's fathers or married men.

"I was an athlete. Olympics before going pro. Sort of the same thing, but different."

"Olympics? Impressive. What was your sport?"

"Track and field."

"I didn't know there was such a thing as professional track and field," I admitted.

"There's professional everything," he countered. "For me, it was mostly sponsorships, and endorsement deals. I even made it onto a cereal box."

"Now that really is impressive. Everyone eats cereal, you must have been a household name."

"Not quite, but thank you."

We passed several rows that were already occupied with parties already settled in for the day. They had cushions and blankets set up to make the chairs more comfortable. I would have to remember to bring a pad for my backside if I came to many more of these.

"This looks good," her dad announced.

We wiggled our way into the row and set up, claiming several seats to either side, as well as seats in the row in front of us. Once we got situated, her dad excused himself to the facilities.

I barely had time to turn around in my seat before Bro was next to me. He appeared suddenly, as if he were a ghost. Something he had never done in my presence before. Today he was decked out in the outfit he would have performed in, a short skirt— more loin cloth than skirt— fringed leggings covered his calves, and he wore a leaf crown. His skin glittered like cut diamonds.

He held his hands out in front of him and flipped his palms back and forth. "If I'm not here, how come I can see myself?"

He looked solid. And the last time I touched him, he had definitely felt solid. But he wasn't. I reached up and took one of his hands. I felt his skin against mine, only now it was cool and not quite substantial. Bro had been such a steadfast presence, it was hard to accept he really wasn't.

"I don't know, Bro. And it would seem that I am the only person who can see you. Addy never saw you. And Emi only noticed you as orbs floating around Collin."

"Why wouldn't Emi be able to see me?" he asked. His

face was so sad. This was hard on him. He had been walking around for years, not realizing he was dead.

I don't know how, or maybe it hadn't been years, and he grew over time. Just because I had been a ghost, it didn't mean I knew how it all worked. I didn't know why I had suddenly been there for Emi, or why I had taken over Addison's body when she had clearly wanted back in, until she realized she really didn't.

"Because you are a ghost. And unlike most people, Emi can see ghosts. She saw me," I said.

"You mentioned Addison, the person you aren't but that's her body. Can you see her?" He looked around as if he were looking for someone.

"My body now. I could see her, talk to her. She's gone now," I said.

He cast his dark eyes at me. They were rimmed in pink. I felt the sting of tears in my own eyes. I reached out and cupped his cheek. His skin wasn't there, something kept my hand from passing through his presence, but whatever was stopping my hand in space wasn't skin.

"Gone, gone?" he asked.

I nodded.

"How?"

I shrugged. "She realized that she didn't have to struggle with this life. She didn't want to be controlled by her mother anymore."

I remembered the look on Addy's face when she realized that she could be well and truly free of this world. She had sparkled, not unlike Bro. Only instead of being sad, she had been euphoric.

"I don't want to go anywhere. I just got you back," his wistful tone cut straight to my heart.

I didn't want to lose him again. But he was already lost to

me. "There isn't a way for us to be together that I can think of," I confessed. "I love you, but I don't see a way forward."

I wiped my cheeks as tears escaped my eyes. I quickly glanced around, looking for Emi's dad. I didn't want him to catch me sitting here crying. That would be really awkward.

"This is the last time we see each other, isn't it?" Bro wiped at his own tears.

As far as breakups went, this one was the first one to truly break my heart. Neither of us wanted it to end.

"Do you need me to leave?" he asked.

I held his insubstantial hand a little tighter. He rested his head on my shoulder. His presence was no longer warm and solid. He was cool and his touch tingled.

"You can stay, as long as you want."

He huffed a half chuckle. "I can't. That's the issue here."

"Right, right."

"Have I missed anything?" Emi's dad asked as he returned and took his seat on the opposite side of me from Bro. He left a few spaces between us.

My gut clenched. How would Bro react to seeing his old friend? How did I continue to navigate this?

"No performances yet. Some of the dance teams have been checking out the stage, and there are some drummers who keep practicing. We're still really early," I said.

"Don't mind me then." He lifted an ereader showing me why he was about to start ignoring me.

I didn't mind. I wasn't up for much of a conversation at the moment. Bro didn't seem to notice his old friend. He didn't seem to be noticing much of anything anymore. Bro and I sat leaning into each other in silence. The announcer opened the event, and the first performance of the day took the stage.

It wasn't long before Bro sat up, forcing me back into my own space.

"I have to go, we're up early in the program." He stood, still holding my hand. He turned and leaned down to me. His lips tingled and were mostly not there as he brushed them against mine. "Goodbye, Mancey."

He sparkled and dissolved into glitter on the air as he walked away. He didn't expand into space the way Addy had, he just faded. I caught glimpses of him on stage, dancing behind Collin. But he really wasn't there. When Collin's dance team performed a second time, Bro wasn't there at all.

33

———

There was something different about knowing Addy's ghost was out there and might pop in for an argument, and having her be truly gone. I knew I technically wasn't alone, I had friends and colleagues. That wasn't the same. I was completely on my own. I was actually lonely.

Brody Nakamura wasn't only just a ghost who abandoned me after an argument, he was no longer even that. There was a physical ache in the difference between heart break and the finality of death. Complete death, not that in between that the ghosts in my life occupied.

I stayed in bed too long the days after the dance competition. I didn't go out to the beach. The ocean didn't have the answers. Not anymore it didn't. Because it couldn't tell me why I couldn't be with Bro. Why did Bro have to be the ghost of some old guy? If he had been alive, I wouldn't have looked at him twice. Or would I? Why did the love of my life have to be a ghost?

I wandered around the small bungalow I had rented. I needed to pack up and leave. I had a place on Oahu for the rest of my break from PIE.

I hadn't expected to run into Collin on Maui. I saw no reason to visit his office on campus and deliver the news regarding my research. I did all of that in Emi's backyard. He now had my official PIE email, he could contact me when he wanted that documentation.

That had been the only real reason I needed to island hop. Well, that and *Cherry Ala Mode* was already scheduled to dock in Honolulu in a couple of weeks. I needed to catch my ride.

I left the TV running in the background for some noise. It was too quiet, and the quiet felt like loneliness.

There was some surfing event going on. And the chatter and banter of the announcers made me not feel so alone. The announcers grew louder and more frantic. I paused in my packing to see if I could figure out what all the excitement was about. The overhead view of a crowded beach cut to underwater footage. There were lots of bubbles and a floating surfboard. I couldn't tell what was going on.

I returned to my folding. I managed to figure out there had been an accident. But the man they seemed to be talking about was on his own feet, walking between two lifeguards. I watched as they took him to a gurney set up in front of an ambulance. The man gave a thumbs up as EMTs placed an oxygen mask over his face.

The announcers continued to speak in rapid, excited tones. The underwater, blurry footage kept popping back up on the screen. The surfer left in the ambulance to get checked out, but he was okay. I stopped paying attention after that. I had to be out of the bungalow in the morning, and I needed to focus on my packing.

In the morning, I had my bags next to the door as I waited for my ride to the airport. As I closed the door behind me, I was overcome with a sense of finality. Unexpected tears ran down my cheeks.

This place wasn't home, but it was the last place where I had been with Bro. And the beach across the street was the last place I had a conversation with Addy. I had come ashore to wrap up Addy's old life, I just didn't realize how much of my new life was entangled in all of that.

The flight wasn't long enough to catch a nap, and whatever flight nerves Addy had bequeathed on me were completely gone. Maui was the end of one chapter, hopefully Oahu would be the start of the next chapter of my life.

The condo I rented for the last few weeks before it was time to rejoin my colleagues on board *Cherry Ala Mode* was a small and functional apartment. It was within walking distance to the beach. I had nothing better to do than sit and watch the waves, or spend the day window shopping.

I found myself journalling. It wasn't a habit I had before all of this happened to me. The therapist I had seen during the few months post recovery suggested it once or twice. But nothing about it appealed to me. Not until I really felt the stabbing pang of Bro's absence.

I had a picture of him on my phone. I had taken it from an old article I found while documenting how my research complemented the work he had started. I wanted to save that picture somewhere. I wanted to draw him how I remembered him, and I wanted to do stupid silly things, like draw hearts around his face, and keep copies of every Pele and Pete cartoon I could find.

I spent too many nights being maudlin and shoving Twinkies into my face while I tried to come to terms with my feelings over cut up magazine pictures. I watched sappy movies that made me cry, and did more damage to the stock of junk food I had bought for the crew than I had realized.

But it seemed to hurt a little less each time I created another page about my broken heart, or my broken life.

I needed to get back to work. I missed my work. I missed my new friends and colleagues. And as much as I missed Bro, I knew I needed to keep my mind occupied so that I didn't spiral into a complete heartbroken depression. I was already in danger of that. If I could have called Strandfield to come pick me up early, I would have. The longer I stayed, the more it felt as if Hawaii wasn't for me anymore.

I had one last shopping trip to get all the glue sticks and stickers, and magazines I would cut up for collage. I may have bought too many craft supplies to take on board. It felt like I bought too much junk food. But everything I bought would run out before long, and I would chastise myself for not having gotten enough.

"Late night arts and crafts?" the cashier asked as I made my last purchase before heading out to the ship in the morning.

"Stocking up for being out in a boat for a few weeks," I admitted.

"I hear you there. Are you sure you have enough of these?" She waggled a box of PopTarts at me.

"I had better." I thought I had a lot of boxes, but now I second guessed my purchase. "Should I get more? I'm buying enough to share. But I'll hoard them if it comes down to it."

I bought more.

34

———————

I was on time, but the boat was late.

That shouldn't have happened. *Cherry Ala Mode* should have been docked by now. I wasn't expected to arrive until closer to cast off time. Maybe I was late? Would Strandfield abandon me if I missed launch time?

The vroom-vroom engine equivalent of a muscle car in speed boat form caught my ear. Strandfield's personal contradiction in environmentalist driving a gas guzzler, *The Sea Dervish*, appeared beyond the breaker wall. A spray of water and waves followed in its wake.

Strandfield wasn't the one driving then. He puttered around like a little old lady Sunday driver when he was behind the wheel. All that horsepower, and he really only cared about the visual esthetics, sleek lines, and passenger capacity. At least that's what it was like whenever I was out on the boat with him. He was not a reckless driver in public. Or at least with an audience.

Strandfield would have an aneurysm if he knew how his precious baby was being handled at the moment.

Strandfield was always courteous around docked boats. This guy didn't care. He was having fun.

I couldn't make out who it was from this distance.

I shaded my eyes, as if cutting the glare from the noon sun would help increase my ability to focus. Even as the boat drew closer, I still didn't recognize the man behind the wheel. There was nothing familiar about him. He was taller than Strandfield, and had a deep tan. After all that time I had spent on the *Cherry Ala Mode*, I pretty much was familiar and on a first name basis with everyone from the ship. I couldn't figure out who this guy was.

The driver slid the boat around like he was drifting something low and fast. The boat moved like it was in charge, and not at the greater mercy of the ocean under it. He began waving at me, pointing me over to a different area where a long walkway jutted into the water. Boats were temporarily moored along the length of the dock. I dragged my bags out to the end, where it was free of parked boats.

The Sea Dervish approached entirely too fast. It twisted around and with a wave of water slid next to the dock. I jumped back, but my feet still got sloshed.

"Who the hell..." I started to yell, and then I got a look at him.

His hair was shaggy and wild, long just to his shoulders. A deep black that barely reflected any light. His skin, a deep dark golden tan, and his smile, that smile cut me straight to my core. I didn't recognize him exactly, but I knew him. Deep in my bones, I knew him.

He jumped from *The Sea Dervish* and looped a rope around the cleat on the dock in a single motion. He stood, brushed his hair away from his brow, and swept me against him in a grand gesture. Like a Hollywood star of old, he swept the sunglasses from his eyes. I felt the recognition wash over me.

"Hi Mancey, miss me?" And then he kissed me.

With a soft sigh, I melted into his embrace and kissed him back. It was Bro. I didn't know how, and at that moment I didn't really care. All that mattered was I had Bro back.

I didn't let him come up for air for a long time. I kept renewing the kiss and holding him tight every time I felt him ease back.

"I guess you did miss me?" he chuckled, when I finally let him go.

"How? Who? Why are you in *The Sea Dervish*? Where is *Cherry Ala Mode*?" I had so many questions.

"You forgot what and when," Bro teased as he tossed my bags onto the boat.

He jumped the small gap and braced with one foot on the dock and the other onboard. He held out his hand and helped me to make the small leap from one surface to the other.

I waited impatiently as he untethered the boat from the doc.

"Are you going to fill me in at all? Or are you going to leave me guessing?"

The new Bro positioned himself behind the wheel and with a smoothness that was only rivaled by Strandfield's careful handling of the boat. Bro started the engine and guided it away from the docks. He no longer handled the boat like a maniac.

"Well?" I prodded when I couldn't take the silence that was building between us.

"Let me get us under way, and then I'll explain everything."

He was infuriatingly calm. Then again, he knew what was going on. I didn't. For all I knew this man was kidnapping me, and I was taken in by his rakish good looks, broad high cheek bones, deep dark eyes, full lips, and dazzling smile. He could have stalked my inner thoughts to know about Bro.

I scoffed at my own musings. That wasn't possible, and I knew this was Bro, just as I knew I wasn't in my first body, he wasn't in his.

I cast my gaze out to the water and let the soft breeze caress my face and mess up my hair. Wherever we were headed, this man wasn't in a hurry. Time moved differently when I was out on the water, and after what probably was a very long time, but felt like the blink of an eye, Bro brought the boat to a stop and cut the engine.

I stood and looked around. There was no ship. We were surrounded on three sides by verdant cliff walls. And the natural harbor waters were relatively calm.

The new Bro finally turned his attention to me. "Now, I can give you all of my attention, away from prying eyes."

He smoldered in a way that turned my bones to jelly.

I was mush in his arms as he enfolded me and claimed my lips. I shouldn't be doing this. I didn't know who this man was. I did, he was Bro, but how? Who had he been?

With remorseful reluctance, I braced my palms against his chest. It was firm. There were some serious muscles hiding under his shirt. I pushed. He didn't budge, but I stumbled back.

He caught me with a gentle hand under my elbow.

"My name is Brody Kawai."

My brows shot up. I never could get this forehead to master the single brow lift.

"No, really, it is. I was a surfer. People called me Bro."

"Was?"

He shrugged. "Okay, technically still am. But no longer at the same level. I grew up surfing, I won't embarrass myself out on the waves. But Kawai, he did competition surfing. Was a pro."

"Was?" I asked again.

"You know you are supposed to move through the rest of the five Ws," he said with an exaggerated huff.

Bro sat on the bench opposite me.

I reached out and took his hand in mine. His fingers were a little rough from work, but his palm was soft, and they were comfortably large as he closed his fingers over mine.

"Okay," I started. "Who are you?"

"Brody Kawai, I'm known as Bro." He pulled his hand away from my grasp and rested his pointer finger in the middle of his chest. "I got rag-dolled on what should have been an easy barrel run. And then I got beaned in the head by my board. It was all caught on camera, too, because I was filming for the sponsor. Which means that all the spectators on shore witnessed it. I've got to tell you, it's weird watching your own death on camera. They resuscitated me on the beach, only it was me, Brody Nakamura, who came to."

I let out a long breath. It sounded so familiar. "Do you know what happened to Brody Kawai? Is he hanging out around you?"

"He left with the dolphins."

"Dolphins? I've never heard that expression before."

"Not an expression, I'm serious. I've seen the footage. We decided to not release it to the public, but it's out there. I mean people with their phones recording the live feed... I can't control that. Anyway, at some point just before the rescue team dragged the body out of the water, you can see the shadow of a dolphin, and then there are two shadows, and they leave."

"Maybe you just couldn't see the second one," I said.

He shook his head vehemently. "No, it may only be a shadow, but it's obviously a single dolphin, and then it's not. There is also a very minor change in the body, like it really let go. I'm guessing Kawai decided there was no coming back from his accident. He saw an opportunity and took it."

"That's good, I guess. I hated fighting with Addy all the time." We were quiet for a long moment, just staring into each other's eyes. I was trying to read into his soul. Could I really trust this?

"Okay, that takes care of who, what, how. When did all of this happen?"

Bro slowly shook his head. "Immediately after I left you at that dance showcase. I can remember thinking, if you could do it, why couldn't I. All I wanted was to stay with you, be with you, and that was never going to be possible unless I did something about it. And then I was gagging up salt water on the beach surrounded by a lot of very concerned people. I stood and waved to a lot of applause and cheering, but I was still whisked away in an ambulance. They kept my butt in the hospital for two days for observations, and then they let me go."

"Only two days?" I practically yelled. "They kept me in for almost a week," I complained.

He shrugged. "I don't know what to say. I was up and out of there. Maybe it was because I pretended I knew exactly what was going on. And I answered when they called me Brody, or Bro, I mean that's my name. But I had to get out of that hospital and find you. Only I couldn't. You were no longer staying at that bungalow. And it wasn't like I could go up to Emi or Collin and ask about you."

"Actually," I interrupted. "You probably could have with Emi. She understands."

"Yeah, but she never lost who she was, even after her accident," he said. "She would think it's weird."

"We can argue about that later. Right now, I need to know how did Strandfield give you his boat?"

Bro chuckled. "Kawai has connections. And when I said I needed to take some time away from a surfboard, no one argued with me. Especially since I got one hell of a concussion, caught on camera. I remembered that you were working with PIE, so I volunteered. My manager turned my first day into a social media blitz, and it got the organization some international recognition."

"You have a manager?"

"I have a manager. Apparently, I'm a sports celebrity. Or I used to be one. If I play my cards right, I'll milk the accident as an excuse, and then I can pull a Mancey, and do whatever I want because I have the funds to bankroll it."

I scoffed, this was unbelievable, except I had been through it. I knew he wasn't lying. "You'll become the spokesman for safety in sports, concussions should be taken more seriously than they are. You might want to feed that angle to your manager."

Bro laughed. "I forgot, you really were in Hollywood, weren't you?"

"I was a bonafide movie star."

"But you've turned scientist."

"Apparently so have you. Mr. Professional Athlete."

"Taking a break for a while at least," he confirmed.

"And right now that means volunteering on an ocean research vessel?"

He stood and pulled me to my feet. His strong arms wrapped around my waist as he held me close. He was leaner in this body, not so much the wall of pure muscle. But there was no denying the strength he possessed.

"Right now that means being where you are, doing what you are doing. And right this moment, it means this." His head lowered and he claimed my lips again.

35

———

As the kiss deepened, I ran my hands under the hem of his t-shirt and over the smooth skin of his back. Our actions grew more frantic and my need to touch Bro increased exponentially. I needed him to touch me. And he was taking too long.

I broke the kiss long enough to drag his shirt over his head.

Bro laughed as he finished taking his shirt off. He had those washboard abs. Bro always had abs, only before they weren't so defined. I could file my nails on this guy.

I fought the buttons on the front of my blouse, and then Bro brushed my fingers out of the way, and he finished unfastening the buttons for me. I couldn't wait to press my skin against his. I tore at the clips on the back of my bra.

My entire body thrummed as I melted against Bro. His touch invigorated every last one of my nerve endings. It wasn't until one of his hands cupped my breast that it occurred to me, we were outside where everyone and their gods could see us.

"People are going to see us," I managed to squeak out.

His entire body shook as he began laughing. "There is no one out here. That's why I parked us here."

"You came here on purpose?"

"Yes, I brought you here to explain everything and seduce you."

"Well, it's working. But if you're going to seduce me properly"—I looked around the area of the boat we were in, it was not conducive to laying down.—"we need to shift to a more comfortable location."

I looked into the dark entry leading down to the berth. The cot down there was not going to fit the two of us. I did my best at covering my breasts with my arm and took Bro's hand before leading him to the front deck of the boat. I'd napped on those cushions plenty of times, they were comfy and roomie.

"I thought you might resist me a little more than this," he chuckled as we carefully stepped over the narrow walkway to the front of the boat.

"You've met me before, Bro. You should know that I would jump at the chance. I'm absolutely in love with you, and now I can have you, really have you in my life. And you went to all the trouble of getting the boat from Strandfield— he never lets anyone borrow the boat— so you could pick me up and seduce me. You're going to have to explain how you did that, but not right now. You went to all this trouble, the least I could do is not make it any more difficult than necessary."

I lowered to the cushions and reached up for Bro, welcoming him into my arms. I squirmed under his heated gaze, a smirk on his lips, his eyes hooded.

His tongue darted out and licked his lower lip.

I copied the motion as I focused on his mouth. I already experienced his proficient kissing skills. Did he remember how to reduce me to nothing but quivering nerves, and desperate need?

Bro dropped his shorts. What breath I had left in my lungs. It all rushed out on a whoosh. The man was glorious. Brody Nakamura had been a beautiful man with a dancer's body. But Brody Kawai had the body of a professional athlete.

"You like the new me?" He held his arms out, putting his body on display.

"I like the man on the inside, but the packaging is quite pretty."

He brushed at his pecs and abs. "It feels weird, but I'm not complaining."

I giggled. "It takes a bit to get used to the new body. I still catch myself in mirrors and forget this is my face."

"But for me, you haven't changed." He knelt next to me, and traced his fingers down the side of my face.

I captured his fingers and kissed them. "You look different, but I can tell it's you behind these eyes."

My view of him blurred as he came in too close to focus. His lips were warm as he pressed them against mine. He kissed like the Bro I remembered. I slid my arms around him. I needed his skin against mine.

His touch was almost hesitant as he skimmed his hands over my skin. I arched up to press my breast against his palm. As he touched me, I couldn't figure out how to touch him. I wanted my fingers threaded through his hair. I wanted to dig my fingers into the hard muscles of his arms. I wanted the feel of his abs pressed to mine.

I grunted in frustration as my leggings were between my

skin and Bro's. He lifted away from me long enough so I could shimmy out of the rest of my clothes so that I could run my legs over his.

With all of his smooth skin against me, I sighed. I had Bro back in my arms. Even though I technically knew the last time he touched me, he hadn't actually been there. But with this man alive and wrapped around me, I couldn't tell the difference. He was Bro, my Bro, and he was here.

He began kissing down my neck and across my chest, as if he was trying to lick and taste every inch of me. I was helpless against him, not that I wanted to do anything else. I needed to be consumed by him. Moans escaped my mouth. Everything this man did to my body felt beyond amazing.

With my nipple in his mouth, Bro slid a hand between us. I was slick with desire, and his fingers slid along my folds. I rocked my hips against his hand, wanting more of his touch. When he found my clit, I pressed my heels against the cushions to press my hips up.

I needed him tighter against me, inside of me. I needed more of him. Clutching at his shoulders, I dragged his face back to mine. I whimpered as the hand between my thighs left. He swallowed my whimpers as he reclaimed my lips. As he shifted, his cock positioned against my sex, replacing his teasing fingers.

I wanted to sing a glory hallelujah when he slid into me. Bro was as perfect as he ever had been. He was mine, and he was back. He was real. We moved together in a perfect rhythm. My nerves were on fire and my core tightened.

My body felt as if I shimmered and exploded all at once. Bro took my body to the brink of orgasm and beyond. I couldn't scream as the air left my lungs. I had to fight and gasp for air. Bro didn't stop as I crashed around him.

His movements grew faster, more frantic. I wanted to laugh as he was driven to the very edge along with me. I didn't know I could be so happy as he roared out his release. I did that to him, just as he had done that to me. It couldn't have been a more perfect reunion between us.

36

___

Laying next to Bro under the open sky as the boat gently rocked with the waves made this the most perfect moment in my life. Any of my lives. I knew I would hold this memory in my heart for the rest of every life I was lucky enough to live.

I skimmed my fingers over his broad chest. It wasn't going to take me any time to adjust to this new body of his. His muscles were leaner, but he was still strong. I might miss the collar tattoo, but this body had other markings related to his heritage that ran down the side of his neck and across one shoulder. His brow was a little thicker, and his hair a little more wild, but he was Bro through and through.

I could have taken a nap in his arms, but we were going to have to get to the ship at some point. The boss was going to miss his boat.

"Where is Strandfield? Why do you have his boat?"

"He's in Europe checking out the RP *Flip*," Bro said.

"The *Flip*?" I thought the RP *Flip* was decommissioned and sitting in dry dock. "But it's not operational."

Bro shrugged. "Maybe not officially."

The RP *Flip* was a funky ship that was spoken of in reverent mythological terms aboard *Cherry Ala Mode*. Shaped like a giant toothbrush, it could sail out to the location of choice like any normal ship. With the flooding of select ballasts the ship literally tipped ninety degrees vertically and turned into an ocean platform.

With the bulk of the ship under water, it was reported to be incredibly stable. And thus useful for conducting more sensitive research and experiments regardless of the temperament of the surrounding ocean waters.

"Apparently, Strandfield is checking it out for PIE. So, when it officially comes back online, PIE gets first dibs."

"He wants to buy it? What about the Cherry?" *Cherry Ala Mode* had become my home. I didn't want to get used to a different ship.

"Naw, DEEP isn't going to sell it. But they will let us borrow it," Bro explained.

"We? You've been volunteering for a couple of weeks, and suddenly you're all 'we,' as if you're a member of PIE," I teased.

"I'm happily another slice," he smirked. "Look, Strandfield and the crew are going to have a hard time getting rid of me as long as you are around. I did this to be with you." He gestured wildly and thumped himself on the chest. "Mancey, I am aware of how rare and beautiful of an opportunity I have been given. Do you think for one moment I'm going to waste my time pursuing other interests?"

He turned me so that I was propped against him, and looking down into his face. His fingers left tickling trails down my back and over my backside.

"I love you Mancey, I go where you go. I will make

myself indispensable to Strandfield. I'm already certified for diving, and I'm handy with a wrench."

"A wrench? I thought you'd be showing off your data crunching skills," I said.

I loved looking into his face. Even though it was technically a new face, it was my Bro who grinned at me.

"I think for a while, I'll be making use of my physical skills."

I giggled as we both rolled, and he positioned himself above me. His skin against mine was pure heaven. And his renewed arousal was hot and heavy against my hip.

"I do like your physical skills," I purred.

"Should I demonstrate?" he asked.

I hooked a foot around his leg and tugged at him, urging him closer. "Please, I think I need a reminder."

His demonstration was as thorough as previously, if not more so. My moans and screams bounced off the tall cliff walls. The boat rocked with the waves and with the motion we created.

In a failed attempt to stretch and roll away from Bro before he collapsed all of his weight onto me, I fell to the bottom of the boat. I landed with a thump and a giggle.

Bro leaned over the edge of the bench to look down at me. "I thought your sea legs would be better than that."

"I've been on land for six weeks. I don't have sea legs. Besides, what legs I have are complete noodles," I confessed. "Your physical capabilities are well appreciated. But you keep doing that to me, I'm not going to be able to walk on land or sea."

Bro sat up and extended his arms to me. "I will be more than happy to assist you with that."

He let out a soft hiss as I climbed to my feet, and he pulled me against him. His fingers delicately touched my shoulders and he sniffed my neck. "I should have put the canopy up. I'm sorry. You're pink, and you don't smell like sunscreen. Time to get you covered up before you get burned."

I laughed. "You sound like Collin, 'put sunscreen on.'" I tried to mock Collin's detached yet gruff tone when he yelled at the bunch of us grad students on the paler side of tan.

"Maybe he was just looking for an excuse to touch you," Bro said as he handed me clothing.

I shook my head. "Collin applied sunscreen like a bricklayer, trowel it on and slap it into place. I think he saw all this skin as a potential incident report. He only has eyes for his lava flows and Leia. I was just another pain in his ass."

Bro pulled on his shorts, no worries of sun exposure on his broad shoulders, and crawled to the other end of the boat. He held up a tube of sunscreen to show me as he made his way back.

He lifted my hair from my neck. "Hold your hair up."

The lotion was cool as he applied it. His large hand was warm and soft as he gently glided and smoothed the lotion over my skin.

Bro's voice rumbled low in his chest. "Fool has no idea what he was missing. This is the best excuse I can think of to touch you all the time."

"No UV rays for me?" I joked.

"Not while I'm around." Bro tapped the tip of my nose with a dollop of sunscreen before pulling me in close.

My arms felt slick as they slid across Bro's chest and shoulders. "I missed you," I confessed.

He lifted one of his brows. It was completely unfair, he was able to do the single brow lift. "Which time?"

I knew what he meant. Did I miss him while I was off

cavorting on *Cherry Ala Mode*, or after he faded from his ghostly existence. "Every time we were apart. I missed you the most when I had to reference your research, and document how my findings supported your work. Not only were you gone from my side, but you were dead. Gone, gone."

"And when I..." he trailed off.

"When you realized what you were, and we couldn't be together, that hurt the most. I thought I'd never see you again." I had to blink at the tears forming. I wanted to see him. "You're real this time, right?"

Bro brushed his thumb across my cheek. "I am very much real this time. As real as you are."

Suddenly I was filled with panic. I had lost him once, more than once, and I couldn't face it if I lost him again. I clutched him tight. "Don't leave me again. I love you. I don't think I'd survive it if you went away ever again."

"Hey, hey, that's not going to happen. I've come back from the dead for you. I'm not going anywhere." His tone was low and soothing as he held me.

"Promise?"

"I promise. I'll do you one better. When Strandfield gets back, let's have him marry us."

"He's not ordained, is he?" I asked.

Bro shook his head. "He's a ship's captain, he doesn't need to be ordained."

My lips were on Bro's before I could say yes. His lips were perfect against mine. I felt all of his emotion and devotion, and I gave him all that I was.

"That's a yes?" he asked with a gasp.

"That's a yes," I cried, and then I kissed him again. "But I'm not changing my name again," I said through laughter and the quick kisses I peppered over his face.

"I think we are who we are finally supposed to be. I wouldn't dream of asking you to become anyone else."

~

Thank you for reading Hidden Gods
and the Second Endings series.
If you missed any of the previous books, you can go back and
start from the beginning with Dead Sexy.

Check out the Johnny Urban spin off that started with Gil and
Peter's imaginations in Dead Sexy.

Same world, all new romances, check out the Rockstars series.
Start with Ballad Ares.

Sign up for Lulu's newsletter to keep up to date with new releases and happenings. And get a free sexy short story.

https://lulumsylvian.com/newsletter/

ALSO BY LULU M SYLVIAN

Check out these other series

Legatum

Paranormal romantic suspense

The World of Wet Waterfalls

Paranormal reverse harem romance

Rockers

Contemporary Rockstar romance

Holiday Strippers

Contemporary, ridiculous, romance

ABOUT THE AUTHOR

Bio-engineered to be the only redhead in a generation of blonds, Lulu feels that "aliens" may actually be the best answer for a life-time of being asked, "Where did you get that red hair from?"

She did not come into writing from years of scribbling words on paper. Her background is rooted in visual arts and making pictures. Encouraged to make those pictures out of words Lulu began writing just to see what would happen. What happened was two full-length manuscripts in three months.

Lulu cannot ride a horse, a motorcycle, spin a hula hoop, or play roller derby. Yes, she has attempted all of those, even if it has been decades since she's been on a horse or a motor-cycle. She embraces the crazy that comes with that one little genetic mutation, and attempts to live up to the reputation that proceeds her. Lulu would like to apologize for her contribution to the hole on the ozone layer from her use of hairspray in the 1980s.

For more information, visit:
www.LuluMSylvian.com

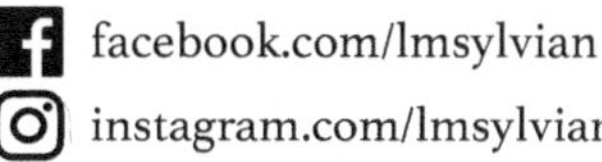